P9-BBP-409

Leith had never been kissed like that

She attempted to push him away, but as his mouth gently closed over hers, she knew that rejecting him was the last thing she wanted to do.

Naylor's hands caressed her back, molding her body against his. ''Oh!'' she gasped, as flames of wanting started to flicker into life, and her arms went up and around him as she freely gave him her lips.

She was in a mindless world where she had forgotten everything about why he was there, when he suddenly stilled. In the next second he had pushed her away from him.

She was still rocking from the unexpected power his kisses had over her when, looking down at her from his lofty height, Naylor mocked, ''Now try and tell me you aren't just anybody's!''

Jessica Steele first tried her hand at writing romance novels at her husband's encouragement two years after they were married. She fondly remembers the day her first novel was accepted for publication. "Peter mopped me up, and neither of us cooked that night," she recalls. "We went out to dinner." She and her husband live in a hundred-year-old cottage in Worcestershire, and they've traveled to many fascinating places—including China, Japan, Mexico and Denmark—that make wonderful settings for her books.

Books by Jessica Steele

HARLEQUIN ROMANCE

HARLEQUIN PRESENTS

HIS
WOMAN

Jessica Steele

Harlequin Books

TORONTO • NEW YORK • LONDON
AMSTERDAM • PARIS • SYDNEY • HAMBURG
STOCKHOLM • ATHENS • TOKYO • MILAN
MADRID • WARSAW • BUDAPEST • AUCKLAND

Original hardcover edition published in 1991
by Mills & Boon Limited

ISBN 0-373-03215-3

Harlequin Romance first edition August 1992

HIS WOMAN

CHAPTER ONE

How many other twenty-two-year-olds stayed in on a Saturday night just listening to the rain hurl itself against the windows? Leith wondered despondently. A moment later, realising she was teetering on the brink of self-pity, she brought herself up short. Good heavens, she thought, since she'd spent most of her life studying, she seldom went out on a Saturday night anyhow!

Determinedly she put her worries and the root cause of her despondency behind her and tried to think more cheerfully. She pinned her thoughts on Rosemary, her friend and neighbour from across the corridor, who came from the same sizeable Dorset village that she did. Why, Leith thought bracingly, were it not for the fact that Rosemary had chosen that weekend to visit her parents in Hazelbury, then Rosemary would probably be in her flat with her drinking coffee right now. True, Travis Hepwood, Rosemary's secret boyfriend, would be with them too, but since Leith liked Travis very much, and felt sorry for the two of them, entertaining Travis as well was no problem.

A fresh blast of heavy rain hit the windowpanes, but this time Leith didn't hear it. Thinking of Rosemary had triggered off memories of that fateful day about a year ago when her brother Sebastian had come seeking her out to say he had just bumped into Rosemary Green—Rosemary Talbot as she now was—in Hazelbury's high street. Rosemary, a year older than Leith, had been Sebastian's school classmate. However, since Rosemary was never allowed to mix with the other children or attend any function after school, no one had ever got to know her really well. To everyone's surprise, though, she had married at eighteen, and had left the village.

Her name had rarely cropped up after that. Then that particular Saturday, Leith's outgoing if slightly irresponsible brother had come to tell her excitedly, 'I've just been chatting to Rosemary Green!'

Leith noted his excitement, but since over-enthusiasm was all part and parcel of his personality, and seldom meant that the house was on fire, she failed to match his enthusiasm. 'She's probably home visiting her parents.'

'That's right!' he agreed. 'She seemed a bit down, actually—nothing you could put your finger on. Anyhow,' he continued in his usual exuberant fashion, 'we were standing right outside Oliphants' Café, so I suggested coffee, and in no time she was telling me how she now lived in London, and had a flat there, and. . .' He paused—and Leith fell into his dramatic trap.

'And?' she queried, even while some part of her was telling her she was going to regret it.

'And she told me that there's a flat going in the block where she lives.'

'Oh, no!' Leith vetoed the idea before he could voice it—though she had to admit that the idea of living and working in London did have tremendous appeal. 'Mother wouldn't go for it, for a start.'

'She would if you told her how you'd look after me—see to it I washed my neck and changed my socks.' Sebastian grinned, just twenty-three then and enjoying to the full the way his mother fussed and worried herself silly over him. 'Anyhow,' he added with endearing honesty, 'I couldn't afford the rent on my own.'

'What if I don't want to go?' Leith tried to stem his impetuosity.

'But you do!' he coaxed. 'You know you do. You didn't disagree with Dad the other day, anyhow, when he remarked that since you'd worked so hard for your qualifications it was a pity that there wasn't a firm around here large enough for you to use them. Now in London. . .'

Sebastian went on in the same vein for quite some minutes. Leith put up several arguments, but he had an answer for every one of them, and soon Leith was starting to feel as excited as he was. She *had* worked hard to achieve qualification in the contracts and purchasing side of engineering, but, in her present job, she was using less than a quarter of her skills.

'There'd be far more opportunities for me too,' he stated. Having dropped out of university, he now worked as a freelance photographer. 'I reckon I've photographed about everything worth photographing around here,' he said, and went back to his 'Now in London. . .' theme until Leith, his enthusiasm infectious, stopped him.

'We'd better go and have a word with Mum and Dad.'

While their father accepted that they were both of an age where they wanted to fly the nest, their mother, who, it had to be said, doted on her son—who'd been a constant source of worry to her—took a little longer.

By Sunday morning, though, they had both their parents' blessing, and Sebastian went off to the Greens' house to get more details of the flat from Rosemary. He returned very crestfallen.

'By Henry, that's a cold household!' he exclaimed. 'Not a smile between the three of them!'

'Rosemary doesn't want you living quite so close?' his mother bridled, having been very much against his going at the start, but now, because he looked so upset, ready to take up cudgels on his behalf.

'She didn't say that,' he replied, the ebullience with which he'd set out for the Greens' household nowhere to be seen. 'What she did say, though, was enough for me to know that Leith and I won't be moving to London.'

'Whyever not?' Mrs Everett demanded.

'Because it turns out that although she's renting her flat while the owners are abroad, the flat that's going opposite her is for sale, not rent.'

'Well, there's more than one flat for rent in London, isn't there?' their father chipped in to declare, and then, with a fond look at his wife, 'And if there isn't, my dear—well, I'm sure, for such a good cause, we could consider letting Leith and Sebastian have the inheritance from their grandfather before they're twenty-five.'

'Could we?' both Leith and Sebastian asked together, the idea of renting accommodation swiftly tossed aside, as it quickly sank in that their father, trustee to the considerable amount of money left to them by his father, seemed prepared to use his discretionary right and let them have it now.

'We'll see,' Mr Everett promised, and from there, with one or two hitches on the way, things had moved relatively quickly.

Because it was sound sense to do so, they looked at other properties for sale. But, once they had seen the flat in the exclusive block where Rosemary lived, no other accommodation bore comparison.

With both Leith and Sebastian in agreement about the flat, they then had to face the fact that although the inheritance from their grandfather was considerable it was nowhere near enough to buy the flat outright.

'We'll get a mortgage like everybody else.' Sebastian refused to be quashed, then found that as he didn't have what was called a proper income he had problems in obtaining a mortgage. 'I'll *get* a proper job,' he dug his heels in to state.

Since Leith would be looking for an employer too—a new employer—she made enquiries, and soon secured an interview for the job of contracts officer with a small firm in London called Ardis & Co.

A month later Sebastian started work at a London

travel agent, living in lodgings on work days, and returning home to Hazelbury on his off days, and Leith heard that she had got the job at Ardis & Co. She was highly delighted, especially when she learned that she had been the only woman called for interview; she had been certain that the job would go to one of the male applicants. She would in fact be taking over from a male contracts officer who would be leaving the company in four months' time.

That her job wouldn't start for three months suited her particularly well. Three months gave her time to give notice on her present job, and, with luck, have funds released from her grandfather's estate, the mortgage secured, and, hopefully, the sale of the flat completed.

All went so well after that that there had just had to be one monumental disaster waiting to happen, Leith later realised. But to start with, four months after she and Sebastian had decided to move to London, they moved into their new flat. The mortgage was crippling, but with both of them working, and with prospects of advancement—which would bring an increase in salary—they were not unduly worried on that score.

They had seen little of Rosemary Talbot during the last four months, so it wasn't until they had been in their flat for a week and Leith went across the hall to invite Rosemary and her husband over for a celebratory drink that Leith learned that Derek Talbot no longer lived there.

'Actually,' Rosemary mumbled, 'my husband moved out.'

Leith wasn't certain then who was the more embarrassed, herself or Rosemary. 'Well, come and have a drink anyway,' she recovered enough to smile.

Only later did she learn that what Rosemary had been doing back in Hazelbury that Saturday when Sebastian had met her had been to come and tell her parents personally that Derek had moved out from the flat they shared and was now living with someone else.

Leith shared many a cup of coffee with Rosemary after that, and although Rosemary seemed reluctant to talk of her marriage at first, it gradually emerged that Derek Talbot was a womaniser who'd treated his wife shamefully. Leith couldn't help feeling extremely sorry for her, especially when she discovered that Rosemary, brought up believing that marriages were forever, could not accept that her marriage was over—even though it had ended up such a disaster and Derek was now asking for a divorce. But her parents were absolutely outraged, being utterly and totally against divorce, and lost no opportunity to tell her so.

Leith and Sebastian had been in their flat a month when Sebastian declared it was time they had a flat-warming party. 'It won't cost much!' he said quickly, as if vaguely aware that Leith was having problems learning her way around the domestic budget.

'Who will we ask?' she questioned, knowing barely anyone in London.

'I've got scads of friends,' Sebastian replied. Besides being the more outgoing of the two, as well as having joined the local drama group, he had lived in London longer.

Leith invited Rosemary, and, when she refused, coaxed her until she accepted, and involved the lonely and unhappy woman in her party preparations, while Sebastian on his part found glasses and brought home liquid refreshment.

If noise meant success, then the party was a success. By eleven o'clock, however, feeling older than her brother rather than younger, Leith wouldn't have minded going to bed. But, as hostess, she had duties to perform. For a start, she hadn't seen Rosemary for fifteen minutes and she did not want her to feel left out.

Aware that the juvenile-seeming bunch of friends which Sebastian had gathered around him might not be Rosemary's cup of tea either, Leith looked round for her.

Hoping against hope that she had not ducked out back to her own flat—not that she'd blame her!—Leith skirted the room until her eyes were drawn to a settee that had been pushed back to the side of the room. There on the settee, looking a little flushed, sat Rosemary. Beside her, in earnest conversation with her, was a man of about twenty-six or -seven, who appeared a good deal more mature than the other male guests. Leith tried to remember his name, recalled that he had been introduced to her as Travis something or other, checked that Rosemary did not appear under stress, and left them to it.

If Rosemary had not been suffering any stress that night, though, it was not long before the situation which had begun with Travis Hepwood became stressful. For Travis, it appeared, had fallen in love with Rosemary at first sight. Leith had a fair idea that Rosemary, against all odds, was similarly affected. The giant problem in their love for each other, though, was the mammoth sense of propriety which had been instilled into Rosemary since childhood. To her it could just not be right that she should love one man while being married to another. And, since she felt unable to divorce Derek, there seemed little chance for her to be happy with Travis Hepwood.

A week later a still very much astonished Rosemary had confided to Leith that she was indeed in love with Travis. In fact, so bowled over was she initially that she had actually gone out to dinner with Travis one night.

'I'm so glad,' Leith replied, knowing from the very few comments Rosemary had let drop that she must have gone through a most unhappy time before Derek had finally left.

'Don't be,' Rosemary answered. 'It was dreadful!'

'You and Travis didn't get on?' Leith, feeling a good deal startled, queried.

'Famously,' Rosemary replied. 'But I felt so guilty— just as if my parents were looking disapprovingly over my shoulder the whole time! Travis phoned last night— I've told him I won't see him again.'

Whatever the strength of Rosemary's convictions about not seeing Travis again, however, see him she did—never by prior arrangement, though, and never in her own flat. For Travis called at Leith's and Sebastian's flat a few nights later—'Just passing and thought I'd pop in,' so he said, which fooled nobody. It happened that on that same night Leith had invited Rosemary to supper. To Leith's way of thinking, it was hardly polite to ask Travis to leave—especially when, by dint of having a small portion herself, she could manage to stretch the food to another plate.

Leith was afterwards about to refuse Rosemary's offer to do the washing-up. Then, 'I'll dry,' Travis volunteered swiftly before she could open her mouth. So Leith left the two of them in the kitchen and found a few tidying-up jobs to do in the dining-room.

After that Travis came to supper regularly. Sometimes Sebastian was there, sometimes he wasn't, but, which- ever way Rosemary's conscience pulled, she—sometimes late, as if having a last-minute tug-o'-war with her upbringing—was always there. So much so that occasionally Rosemary would insist on cooking supper and bringing it over—always with enough for an extra helping in case a guest should turn up. For his part, Travis, who worked in his father's wine-importing busi- ness, always brought some superb wine.

'What gives?' enquired Sebastian, coming home late one night to find Leith barring his way to the kitchen.

'Rosemary and Travis are in there,' Leith replied.

'So?'

'In case you haven't noticed, they're in love.'

'So what's the matter with Rosemary's flat?'

'Rosemary doesn't want to entertain Travis there.'

'Whyever not?'

'It's—not—circumspect,' Leith told him, while wondering at her brother's lack of sensitivity.

'It's crackers!' was his opinion.

Leith afterwards supposed she should have realised that that state of affairs could not go on indefinitely without someone getting hurt. Yet with Rosemary still refusing to go out with Travis and Travis falling more and more in love with her the whole time, there was no way he could stay away. Leith had grown fond of both of them, and, feeling sorry for them, she knew at the same time that this was something they would have to work out for themselves.

Then one night Travis arrived, keyed up at the thought of seeing Rosemary again. Sebastian was home too that night, and chatted amiably with him while Leith did a few 'finishing off' chores in the kitchen. When everything was ready and Rosemary was later than usual, Leith could stand Travis's anxious glances at the door no longer.

'I'll just go and see what's holding Rosemary up,' she said, and went across the corridor to Rosemary's flat. She rang the bell, and waited.

It took Rosemary about a minute to answer the door, but, as all the flats in the building were of the same layout, Leith's 'Ready?' query never got said. For over Rosemary's shoulder she saw at once beyond the short width of the hall and into the sitting-room—and Rosemary was doing some entertaining herself.

Somehow, though, Leith's sensitivity picked up a strained atmosphere as she pulled her glance back from the stocky man who had taken it into his head to start walking over. Something, something in her friend's tense attitude seemed to say that she didn't want her visitor to know she was expected elsewhere.

'Er—sorry to bother you, Rosemary.' Leith thought on her feet. 'I didn't—er—know you had company.' She smiled as the stocky man ambled up to them.

'Aren't you going to introduce me?' he enquired shortly of Rosemary, while his eyes made a meal of Leith's thick chestnut-coloured hair and her beautifully structured face and figure.

'Of course,' Rosemary replied. 'Leith is the new owner of the flat opposite. Leith, my husband, Derek.'

Leith shook hands with him, but cared not at all for the way he ogled her the whole time. 'Er—I won't stay, Sebastian's waiting to be fed,' she said. 'I just wondered—have you any Worcester sauce I can borrow?'

Both Travis and Sebastian looked askance when she returned, without Rosemary but carrying a bottle of sauce. 'Where's Rosemary?' Travis asked at once. Desperately Leith racked her brains, but there was nothing she could tell him, only the truth.

'She's not coming,' she replied, and she and Sebastian had to almost physically restrain him when she revealed that Rosemary's husband was with her.

Having got Travis sitting down again, Sebastian mixed him a stiff drink, and the evening went generally from bad to worse, with Sebastian the only one with any appetite for the meal Leith had cooked. When Travis seemed in need of another stiff drink, Sebastian served him liberally and, Travis's tongue more free than it had ever been, he spoke of his love for Rosemary, his wish to marry her, but how because of her sense of propriety she wouldn't even let him take her out, or so much as mention her name to his family. Much less, when he wanted the world to know of his love, would she allow him to introduce her to his parents.

By the time eleven o'clock ticked round Travis had started to slur his words, and Leith had grown quite cross with Sebastian for so freely upending the bottle each time Travis's glass came anywhere near empty.

'Strewth, you're sloshed!' Sebastian exclaimed when Travis, deciding he was going home, got rockily to his feet and started swaying.

'I don't think it's a good idea for Travis to drive home in that condition,' Leith told her brother coldly.

'I've been drinking too—I'm not driving him!' Sebastian declared. 'Anyhow, he lives somewhere in darkest Essex, so lord knows what time I'd get to *my* bed—even supposing he can remember where he lives. He can doss down on the couch.' He decided on the easiest of all the alternatives.

'What about his parents?—they'll worry,' protested Leith, remembering the occasions when Sebastian hadn't come home at night, and how her mother had gone almost hairless.

'Hell, Leith, he's pushing thirty! It won't be the first time he's spent a night on the tiles!'

So Travis stayed the night on their couch, with the only bonus for him being that, bleary-eyed and hung-over the next morning, he had a chance to have a brief word with Rosemary before she went to her computer programmer's job. The upshot of that, though, was that Travis felt worse than ever on learning that Derek Talbot had called to again ask Rosemary for a divorce, but that Rosemary had given Derek an outright 'no'. And if that wasn't a big enough blow to Travis's hopes, Rosemary, in the cold light of morning, told Travis that she would not be accepting any more invitations to the flat opposite for supper either.

Rosemary said more or less the same thing to Leith when next she saw her, and Leith realised she could not interfere, but just be there when Rosemary needed a friend.

She still saw Rosemary, and had coffee with her on many occasions, and Travis came to their flat occasionally too—Leith knew on the offchance of seeing Rosemary. Travis, however, was starting to look haggard, and Leith had been sorely tempted, the last time he came, to contact Rosemary. She'd checked the impulse when she realised that since Travis was being man enough not to ask that of her she really could not interfere, only for Rosemary to reiterate all she had told Travis before.

Then Sebastian started talking in terms of giving up his job, and Leith had something else to worry about. If Sebastian wasn't working, how was he going to pay his share of the mortgage? Then, to prove that troubles never came singly, a disaster occurred when, through none of her own doing, she lost her own job.

She could hardly believe it. She was hardworking and industrious, and in her work as a contracts officer enjoyed the challenge of getting value for money when it came to servicing the needs of the company's departments. She worked mainly with men, and got on with most of them, but she did not enjoy it when Alec Ardis, the son of the firm's owner, one day came into her office and, without any encouragement from her and despite his married status, made an assault on her and refused to take 'no' for an answer. Afterwards Leith could not help wondering if perhaps, with more experience of men, she might not have handled it better. As it was, she became more and more incensed as she tried to break out of his limpet-like hold, the result being that when she did manage to break free she was so outraged—just because she was a female contracts officer, the boss's son thought he could do as he liked with her—that she verbally tore into him.

Very much shaken as she was by the assault, she nevertheless would not have voluntarily given up her job—but she did not get the choice. Unfortunately, Mr Ardis senior had been passing when her furious 'lecherous, cretinous, oversexed reptile!' rent the air. She was still giving forth when he came in to investigate.

Leith felt sick to her stomach when Mr Ardis, either not believing that his son had just pounced unencouraged on her, or perhaps covering up for his son's weaknesses, told her that a month's severance pay would be sent to her, and dismissed her on the spot.

She was still in shock from the assault and everything that had followed when that evening she went on impulse and rang Rosemary's doorbell. 'Are you making coffee, by any chance?' she queried.

'Come in,' Rosemary promptly invited, and opined, 'You look worse than I feel. What's wrong?'

'I've been given the sack,' Leith told her shakily, and, over coffee, gave her a blow-by-blow account.

In Rosemary's book, 'lecherous, cretinous, oversexed reptile' was too polite a term for a man who seemed to think any female working for his father was fair game. 'You should have hit him,' she said, equally outraged on Leith's behalf.

'I might have done if I could have got my arms free,' Leith replied, and took another sip of her coffee.

They sat in Rosemary's neat and tidy sitting-room, and Rosemary commiserated with Leith, voicing the opinion, 'Of course, something like what happened today was bound to happen sooner or later.'

Startled, Leith stared at her. 'I'm not with you,' she stated.

'You're too. . .' Rosemary searched for a word, then to startle Leith further '. . .glamorous,' she brought out.

'Glamorous!' Leith exclaimed, her green eyes shooting wide.

'You've no idea, have you?' Rosemary said gently, and went on to shake Leith some more. 'What with your fantastic chestnut hair, beautiful eyes and skin, not to mention a figure that curves in all the right places, it was a foregone conclusion that some egotistical snake would chance his arm before too long.'

'Good heavens!' Leith murmured faintly. To hear Rosemary tell it, it sounded as though she'd been lucky to reach twenty-two without some vainglorious male trying it on.

'What you need to do, Leith, is to try and deglamorise yourself a bit.' Rosemary smiled, and their talk went on, until Leith spoke of the urgency of finding another job.

'I can't afford not to work, not with the whacking mortgage repayment Sebastian and I have to find every month,' she confided.

'Don't I know it!' Rosemary agreed, and revealed, 'If the rent on this place wasn't paid until the end of the year, I'd be in trouble myself. As it is, I'm saving like mad to have something in the kitty when next rent day comes round. But, to get back to your problem, I shouldn't think you'll have much difficulty getting another job, will you?'

'My qualifications bear scrutiny,' Leith answered, 'but what do I do for a reference? I can't see Mr Ardis talking of my work in very glowing terms.'

'I can't see him being anything other than honest about your work—not unless he wants to leave himself wide open for you to sue him,' Rosemary stated firmly.

A week later, having applied for jobs with three firms, Leith heard that two of the vacancies were filled, but she was lucky in the third in that she was called for interview. She had by that time, however, had a whole week in which to do quite a lot of thinking. Her thoughts centred in the main on some of the comments Rosemary had made. Leith supposed she must still be feeling shaken at being grabbed at by Alec Ardis, and more than a touch bruised by her dismissal, and the unfairness of it. But even so, even though she was sure Rosemary must be exaggerating, her remarks about her being too glamorous in relation to her work place nagged away at her. Never did she want a repeat performance of being locked in the octopus grip of Ardis junior—the memory of it was giving her nightmares.

'Sebastian,' she addressed her brother the night before she was due to present herself at G Vasey Ltd for interview, 'I don't suppose you still have those specs you wore when you played a professor in——'

'My last public appearance, you mean,' Sebastian chipped in grandly, referring to his non-speaking part in his drama group's last production. 'As a matter of fact. . .'

Leith hardly recognised herself the next day when, with her usual free-flowing locks fastened severely in a knot at the back of her head, she donned a pair of plain glass, horn-rimmed spectacles, and surveyed the result.

As deglamorisation exercises went, she thought she had done very well. But, while her non-dramatic soul was saying that to present herself at Vasey's looking the way she did was going a bit over the top, she had never been dismissed from a job before. She had been accepted for the job at Ardis & Co, looking the way she normally looked, but if to keep her job—and she had no idea at that stage whether there was a Vasey junior, or similar, at G Vasey Ltd—she had to go in for a bit of deglamorisation, then so be it.

Leith's interview at G Vasey Ltd went well, to her surprise, no one being a bit suspicious or in any way questioning about the thick-framed glasses she wore. She took them off the minute she entered her apartment block, realising that since no one at Vasey's had seen her without her glasses they had no need to question why she was wearing them now.

She then had two painful weeks to sit it out while she waited to hear if she had got the job. In the meantime she applied for other jobs too, but it was the one with G Vasey Ltd that she wanted. For one thing, it paid better than she could believe, and for another the work seemed to be something she could really get her teeth into. There was a fair indication too that, if she got the job, she was going to work harder than she had ever worked, in that she would have an assistant to work with her.

The news that she had in fact been successful in her interview went a very long way to ease her bruised feelings—so much so that when the day dawned when she was to start her new job she almost forgot to pull her hair back into a screwed-up knot, and to don her glasses.

In time, though, she remembered the way it had to be. Suitably deglamorised, even to the extent of hiding her shapeliness beneath loose-fitting garments, she made her way to G Vasey Ltd, where she spent a morning being shown to her office, and being introduced around the contracts and purchasing department. In particular she made the acquaintance of Jimmy Webb, her seventeen-year-old assistant, who she quickly realised was a mine of information about absolutely everything that was going on.

It was from Jimmy that she heard the worrying news that Vasey's had recently been bought out some months ago by the giant Massingham Engineering. Her immediate thought was to be much concerned about her job, and then very much concerned that, without this splendidly paying job, she would be unable to pay her share of the mortgage.

'Will—um—any of the Massingham staff be moving

here, do you know?' she asked Jimmy, trying desperately not to be alarmed, but, well schooled in dealing with the profitability side of company business, unable to see Massingham's keeping on Vasey staff if they had their own people able to do the work.

'Massingham's are moving their whole business up north,' the knowledgeable Jimmy informed her. 'Plant, offices, the lot. According to the grapevine, working on the sound economics of the move north, Massingham's have already sold their works here, and the only staff transferring will be those needing a London base.'

Leith's spirits, which had instantly lifted, at once plummeted. 'What staff would they be?' she queried, striving for a casual note.

'None but the top brass, so I gather, Miss Everett,' Jimmy told her cheerfully. 'And not for ages yet. In fact, not until the building extension at the back is completed and all the offices are wall-to-wall carpeted.'

As relief washed over her—top brass she was not!—a touch of whimsy smote her. 'Did you learn what colour the carpet will be?' she teased her assistant, saw him grin cheekily, and added, since she was only five years older than him, 'My name's Leith. Now fill me in on a few of these files.' Jimmy was smiling happily as he pulled his chair up alongside her desk.

In no time Leith was getting on famously at the new Massingham Engineering acquisition—which was apparently, for the moment, to keep its G Vasey Ltd name. There had been a tremendous hash made of one contract by her predecessor, it was true, but that had all but been completed when it had landed on her desk, so there was no way she could be held to account for it. Even Dave Smith, a senior contracts officer, had agreed that. Though Leith, with her high sense of responsibility, would much rather that the Norwood & Chambers file had landed on somebody else's desk.

Life for Leith settled down to a pleasant pattern. At work, given that, despite her *de*glamorisation, she had had cause to cold-shoulder one Lothario from Purchasing and another from Sales who had been fresh beyond what she thought acceptable, she was quite contented with her lot. She worked hard, and she earned the rewards.

Life at home was pleasant too. Her social life was not outstanding, but, having the reverse of her brother's outgoing personality, she preferred to make friends slowly. And, thinking of friends, her friend Rosemary seemed to be suffering in the same way as Travis Hepwood. Though it was a chance meeting with Travis when he called at the apartment block, ostensibly to visit Leith and Sebastian, when the two bumped into each other.

Rosemary later confessed to Leith that seeing Travis looking so haggard had really got to her. It must have done, Leith realised, for Rosemary was still taking the greatest pains that not so much as a whiff of the fact that she might care for someone else got out. Her biggest fear was that any hint that she might have formed an attachment for someone else would see her husband not waiting for her to agree to a divorce, but scandalising her parents by attempting to do the divorcing himself. Yet, given her great fears on that score, Rosemary, when she knew full well that Travis was in their flat, came across the corridor for coffee later that night.

After that, while never again did she stay long enough to have supper—or do the washing-up—Rosemary, still popping across to Leith's and Sebastian's flat at any time, accepted about two invitations in particular each week for coffee. Travis was, without fail, always there too.

Leith had been at G Vasey Ltd for two months when Sebastian, with his usual exuberance, came home from his travel agent's job and told her that he was flying off to India on Friday for a holiday.

'India!' Leith exclaimed. This was the first she'd heard of it.

'Heavens, Leith, it's only a nine-hour flight away! I'll be back in two weeks.'

'So have a good time,' she told him, recovering, and went to help him pack. . .

Another sharp blast of heavy rain threw itself at the windowpanes of her flat, and brought Leith, startled, out of the brown study she had fallen into. She flicked a glance at her watch. Heavens, it was gone ten o'clock! She must have been sitting there reviewing the happenings of this last year for an age.

Leaving her chair, she went to the kitchen and set the kettle to boil for a warm drink, while her thoughts drifted back to what had started her on the trail of looking back. It didn't take much thinking about. The root cause for her worry, for her looking back instead of forward, was her dear brother Sebastian and how, a week ago, as casual as could be, considering his name was on the mortgage agreement the same as hers, she had received a postcard from him. 'India's great—staying on. Know you'll manage.'

At first she was furious that he could be so careless of his responsibilities for half of the mortgage. It was a foregone conclusion that he wouldn't be sending his half by post, by bank, or by any other means. Then she had telephoned her parents, and learned that they too had heard from Sebastian. Leith knew then, when her mother began, 'Isn't it exciting?' that she was wasting her time expecting her to agree that it was about time Sebastian got his act together. 'He'll be able to take marvellous photos while he's in India, won't he?' her mother had gone on, and only at the tail-end of their conversation did she think to mention their mortgage. 'Naturally, he's seen to it that his commitments are met, hasn't he, dear?'

For her mother, the sun rose and set with Sebastian. Leith at that moment saw no point in putting her in a position where she would have to defend him—which she would. Nor, when their parents had already helped them more than enough with furniture and carpets and the like when they had first moved in, did she think she could take any more from them. They, like everybody else, had other calls on their money, and it just wasn't on that they should be asked to pay Sebastian's heavy share of the mortgage.

So she said lightly, 'You know Sebastian,' knowing full well that her mother, wearing the rosiest of rose-coloured glasses about her only son, would think that her only daughter had answered in the affirmative.

The kettle boiled; then, just as Leith was going to make a cup of chocolate, there was a ring at the doorbell. Why she should immediately think it might be Sebastian, when he had his own key anyway, she didn't know. Worry about finding his half of the mortgage must be getting to her, she realised as she left the kitchen, knowing that just thinking of her brother was not going to conjure him home to pay his dues.

She opened the door—it was not Sebastian. 'Travis!' she exclaimed. He looked terrible and, from the way he clutched at the doorpost for support, drunk. Then she noticed that he was also soaking wet. 'Come in,' she invited, for she could do nothing else.

She helped him to the kitchen, as that seemed to be the best place for him for the moment, and sat him down at the kitchen table while she went and got a towel.

'Did you walk here?' She attempted some light-hearted questioning, as he dabbed at his face and hair with the towel she had handed him. To her mind it was inconceivable that he had driven here in such a state.

'I've been standing outside for ages—wanting to come in, but knowing I shouldn't.'

'Rosemary's not here this weekend,' Leith told him gently. 'She's gone to her parents'.'

Travis heaved a tremendous sigh. 'That figures,' he replied, and suddenly his face was working as though he was having a mighty battle not to break down. A few moments later he had regained control, but it was clear that he was still dreadfully upset when he revealed, 'Yesterday—everything seemed to bubble up inside me and, and I thought—I thought I couldn't cope any more with a relationship that wasn't a. . .with loving someone who I knew loved me but who was, because of her upbringing, her beliefs, her parents, convention—fear of scandal—propriety—you name it, I went through the lot yesterday.'

Leith took the towel he had rolled into a ball from him and decided that a cup of strong black coffee might not come amiss. She was busy with cups and saucers as more words poured from his liquor-loosened tongue. She placed a cup of coffee in front of him, but Travis was still letting go with everything that had been tearing away at him ever since he had first clapped eyes on Rosemary. Leith wasn't embarrassed, just saddened that his love for her friend had brought him to this, as he revealed how, for fear of losing what little chance he had with Rosemary, he had kept quiet about his love when he'd wanted to shout it from the rooftops. How, more than anything, he'd wanted to tell his family all about her, but how, because Rosemary had shrunk away from him in horror at the very idea, he had given her his solemn promise that, outside this building, her name would never leave his lips.

'Then yesterday, when I felt I was going to go mad if I didn't get something settled, I rang her and said I must see her privately.' He was silent then for long moments, clearly far, far away.

'But Rosemary wouldn't see you alone?' Leith guessed.

He shook his head. 'Idiot that I was, I was crass enough to insist, since I couldn't see her privately; to push her into a corner and tell her. . .tell her—oh, lord, I must have been mental!—that if I couldn't see her privately I wouldn't see her ever again.'

'Oh, Travis!' Leith said sympathetically, and just had to ask, 'What did Rosemary say?'

'Nothing,' he replied shakily. 'She just put the phone down, and I knew,' he drew a shaky breath, 'that it was all over.'

'I'm sorry,' was all she could think of saying. Then Travis was rousing himself and, his coffee untouched, was mumbling something about getting back to Essex. 'Where's your car?' she asked in sudden alarm, as he lurched to his feet and took a couple of unsteady steps across the kitchen.

'Outside—I think,' he answered.

More rain hit the windowpanes, and Leith came to a decision. It was definitely not a night to let a friend wander around in a drunken stupor searching for his car. And, should he chance to find it, it was little short of criminal, the state he was in, to allow him to drive it.

'I think you'd better rest here for a while,' she followed him out of the kitchen and into the sitting-room to tell him. She thought, as what she said registered and he looked towards the couch, that he looked grateful, and wondered if he was vaguely remembering that the last time he'd been plastered he had spent the night on that same couch. 'Oh, I think we can do better than that this time,' she told him, as she steered him from the sitting-room and along the hall and into Sebastian's bedroom.

Fifteen minutes later Travis was sleeping like a baby. She had helped him out of his jacket, tie and shoes, reckoned he wouldn't come to any great harm if he slept in his damp shirt and trousers, and placed a duvet over him. She hung his jacket on a hanger on the hat-and-coat fixture next to the deerstalker hat that Sebastian invariably donned when he went out, but which he had left behind when he'd gone to India.

Five minutes went by as she reflected that Rosemary must be feeling as miserable as Travis, then, checking to see that Travis was all right as she passed, she went to bed. It had not been such a dull night after all, she mused, hoped Travis's head wouldn't be too sore in the morning, then found that, whatever diversions might occur, once the excitement was over she was back to worrying about the wretched mortgage.

In an attempt to think about something else, Leith thought about her job at Vasey's, and how fortunate she was to have Jimmy Webb as her assistant. Thoughts of Jimmy, however, brought the reminder of how on Friday he had brought the news—gospel, so he said, after so much rumour—that the top brass from Massingham's were moving into the newly completed extension on Monday. And that was not all. According to Jimmy, Mr Massingham himself, the owner of the whole Massingham empire, would be moving in too.

Leith doubted that she would ever meet the man in such a highly exalted position. All she hoped was that her job was as secure as everyone had led her to believe. It would be a poor look-out on *her* share of the mortgage, let alone Sebastian's, if she lost this job that paid so well.

She had drifted off, and had been fast asleep for some hours when the sound of someone's keeping their finger pressed on her doorbell roused her from a deep sleep. Still half asleep, her brain only semi-functioning, she left her bed and, pulling a robe about her as she went, switching on lights in her wake, she went to stop the incessant din.

'What the dickens is going on?' she demanded angrily of the tall, dark-haired stranger who stood there.

Unanswering, he removed his finger from the bell and stared unsmiling down at her, then at her thick tousled chestnut hair, her beautiful skin, still flushed from sleep. He scrutinised her perfect features, his all-assessing gaze moving to her shape, clearly outlined as she pulled the folds of her cotton wrap closer to her. He finished off his unhurried inventory by taking in her bare and dainty toes.

But Leith, who could not remember ever being put under such an itemising microscope before, had had enough. 'Goodnight!' she snapped, and went to slam the door shut on him—then found that his foot was in the way. 'What. . .' she began as, fully awake by then, she felt fingers of fear begin to nip.

'I'm looking for Travis Hepwood,' the tall man grated, and, for all there appeared a world of aggressiveness about him, the fact that he knew Travis somehow eased her fear.

'Travis. . .' She broke off, her customary reserve nowhere to be seen. She felt suddenly protective of Travis, who was in no state whatsoever to defend himself if this man, for some reason, meant to set about him—which looked likely from his manner. 'Why?' she asked sharply, and when that gained no answer, 'Who are you?' she questioned abruptly.

She did not get to learn her late-night caller's name, but felt a touch easier when he bit out, 'I'm his cousin,' and sent any remaining doubts and fears away when he added, 'In case you're interested, his mother's halfway demented worrying about him. I'm here on her account.'

Instantly Leith's thoughts flew to her own mother and how, should she ever see Sebastian looking as drawn and haggard as Travis had been just lately, she would more than likely be halfway demented too. 'You'd better come in,' she said, and stepped back into the hall. The man, somewhere in his mid-thirties, she guessed, stepped into the hall. She saw his eyes go to the coat fixture, and guessed that he knew the jacket hanging there belonged to Travis when he went and took it from its hanger.

'Where's your bedroom?' he rapped shortly.

Leith's mouth fell open in surprise as she realised that this awful man thought she and Travis were sleeping together. It was then, when she thought about it, that she decided that she was just a little fed up with the bossy brute. All she'd done was to try and help Travis a little at a very bad time in his life, and just look at the aggravation she was getting for her trouble!

'Who says he wants to leave?' she hurled back, realising from the way he had taken Travis's jacket that he intended to take Travis with him.

His cousin, she was quickly realising, though, was a man who had an aversion to answering any but selected questions. His chin was jutting with yet more aggression, at any rate, as, ignoring that question, he asked one of his own.

'Are you seriously interested in Travis?' he demanded.

Pinned suddenly by the man's dark gaze, Leith was all at once certain that Travis's cousin had made up his mind in advance that she was more interested in Travis's financial status than Travis himself. And that made her angrier than ever. With difficulty, though, she hid her ire—and it seemed a good idea then to reply to this high and mighty man with what he all too clearly wanted to hear.

'I haven't any serious plans to marry him, if that's what you're asking,' she told him as levelly as she could, and had the hardest work in the world in hanging on to her temper when his glance flicked from her through the open door into her sitting-room. Her carpets, she felt, were noted; so too were the furnishings. As no doubt also the expensive area where the flat was situated had already been registered.

Her fury with the diabolical man nearly went into orbit, though, when, once more pinning his dark-eyed look on her, he drawled, 'Just hanging on to him while he's good for the rent, is that it?' and, having made up his mind to that, seemed not to require an answer.

Leith gave him one just the same. 'I'm not renting it—I'm buying it!' she snapped. And, never having met such an abominable man, she actually heard herself telling him just how large the mortgage on the apartment was, and, while she was recovering from having actually told him something she regarded as no one's business but her own, and was taking another breath to rage on, he got in first.

'You have a private income?' He seemed to think he had a right to know.

'I work!' Leith snapped, sparks flashing in her green eyes as she stared hostilely up at him. 'I work, and darned hard, for every penny I receive!'

Arrogantly he stared down into her upturned, flushed face, then loftily and succinctly he drawled, 'I bet you do!'

Never had Leith come so close to hitting a man. While she still could she turned swiftly round and went marching away to Sebastian's room. Travis's cousin followed her. Abruptly she switched on the light. Travis stirred in his sleep at the sudden light in the room and opened one bleary eye. But Leith's glance went from him to where, at some time in the night, he must have become too hot and in stupor had shed his clothes, which were now in a crumpled heap by the side of the bed.

Her glance was drawn back to the bed again when, clearly befuddled, and with no idea how he came to be where he was, he slurred, 'How did I get here?'

'The condition he's in,' the man by her side immediately assessed his cousin's state, 'I shouldn't think he was much good to you last night.' Leith again came close to physically lashing out at him, and might well have, she realised, had not the object of her aim moved forward to the bed. 'Time to go home, old son,' she heard him say kindly to Travis.

She took herself off to the kitchen, saw with some incredulity from the kitchen clock that it was four o'clock—and shut herself in. She was soon forgetful of the time, however, her thoughts swiftly going back to the man who had put his finger on her doorbell at that hour in the morning, and kept it there.

It was obvious from the way the odious man had spoken to Travis that there was a bond of family caring there, but that in no way excused his manner to her. How dared he speak to her as though she was some trollop with her eye to the main chance!

Feeling fury begin to soar in her again, she determinedly stayed where she was when she heard sounds that indicated that both men were leaving. While it was sad that, from what Travis had said about everything with Rosemary being all over, she too might never see him again, she felt nothing but joy that she was not going to see his overbearing cousin again either.

Keeping her ears open, she heard the outer door open, then close. Releasing a pent-up breath, only then did she realise that she was actually physically tingling from her encounter with the man who had called to collect Travis.

CHAPTER TWO

AFTER a shortened night, Leith got out of bed on Sunday half inclined to believe that she had dreamt the happenings of four o'clock that morning. She took a look into Sebastian's room. His bed had been slept in, but there was no sign of Travis. She had dreamt none of it.

She got on with her day, but her thoughts kept returning to Travis's cousin. Dear heaven, what a man! Dreams about him would surely be of the nightmare variety! She remembered how she had ridiculously thought meeting him had left her tingling, and was then able to scoff at such a fanciful notion. If she had been tingling at all, it had been from fury.

To her annoyance, she was still thinking about the wretched man when lunchtime came and went. From what he'd said, she gathered that he had come looking for Travis at Mrs Hepwood's behest. But how in creation had he known where to look? From what Travis had said, she had gathered that he'd cut his tongue out before he would tell a soul where Rosemary lived. Though it hadn't been to Rosemary's flat that the tall dark-haired man had come, but hers! He was certain too, she recalled crossly, that she and Travis were bedfellows. Detestable creature!

Leith was still wondering what brilliant sense of direction had brought the aggressive male to her door when, in the late afternoon, an extremely apologetic Travis called. He looked ghastly, she thought, as she invited him in.

'I'm not stopping,' he told her quickly, entering her sitting-room none the less and, at her suggestion taking a seat. 'I've come to collect my car, but I just couldn't drive off without first coming up to apologise for my behaviour last night.'

'Your behaviour was fine,' Leith smiled, her heart going out to him. He was now quiet, dignified, and obviously hurting badly inside. He had been slowly emotionally battered ever since he had met his beloved Rosemary.

'You're kind,' he replied, but with no answering smile. 'I was a little off my head, of course, but bits keep coming back.' He seemed to go from her for a moment, then he recollected where he was. 'I suppose I must have been half off my head, without the booze, since Friday when Rosemary finished with me.'

By then Leith was feeling more than a shade guilty that she was the one responsible for the two having met. She would dearly have liked to have told him she was certain that Rosemary had not finished with him. But she was not certain. Rosemary loved him, she was certain of that, but Rosemary was in a particular hell of her own, her love for Travis warring with the convictions she had grown up with.

In the absence of feeling able to make any encouraging remark about the future of his and Rosemary's love for each other, though, Leith opted to ask a fairly negative, 'Are you feeling any better today?'

'How do I look?' he questioned, and almost smiled that time as he followed on, 'No, don't answer that! According to my mother, even the cat wouldn't drag me in.'

'Your mother's been very worried about you,' Leith remarked, having good occasion to remember that, were it not for Mrs Hepwood being nearly demented with anxiety she would never have had his vile and lofty cousin insisting she answered his summons at her door at close to four in the morning.

'I'm her youngest son,' Travis replied, as though to explain why his mother should worry so about him.

'You've a brother?' Leith enquired, silently wondering why, in that case, his cousin had been the one to come calling.

'I've got two, as a matter of fact, Hugo and Will, but they're both married and with responsibilities to their own families. My father's great, but for some reason we have an abrasive effect on each other in a crisis. Which is why, when my mother needed help with regard to me, she naturally contacted Naylor.'

'Naylor's your cousin—and a bachelor?' questioned Leith, still trying to work out why 'Naylor' had 'naturally' been the one Mrs Hepwood had sent for.

'That's right,' Travis agreed, 'though he's more like another brother to me,' he added, and went on to explain, 'His parents were killed in an accident the year I was born. My mother was very attached to her sister, Naylor's mother, and insisted, apparently, that he should live with no one but us.'

'Oh, I see.' Leith thought she'd got the 'naturally' angle. 'Naylor still lives with you, and when your mother——'

'My mother would be horrified if he didn't regard Parkwood as his home, but he's got a flat in London now—though he still comes home occasionally, and regularly rings Parkwood to check if everybody's all right.' Leith was having difficulty in equating this caring-sounding Naylor with the aggressive brute she had tangled with last night when Travis revealed, 'But it was my mother who rang him on Friday and, it seems, confessed—something I'd been too preoccupied to have noticed—that she'd been worried about me for some while. Naylor drove to Parkwood that night.'

'You saw him on Friday evening after you'd rung Rosemary.'

'No, I didn't,' Travis denied quietly. 'I can't say with any certainty where I did go, but it wasn't home. Anyhow, all this time Naylor was trying to tell my mother that I was a big lad now, but when I didn't turn up all day Saturday, he and my father had their work cut out in trying to calm her. When midnight came and I still wasn't home, Naylor came looking for me.'

'You'd told your mother about Rosemary——'

'Lord, *no*!' Travis butted in, horrified. 'Rosemary's so uptight about anyone, in particular family, knowing about us that I've had to keep her name a closely guarded secret. With my father being positive that I've got no problems at work, though, they've guessed, of course, that there's a lady involved, but——'

'But,' Leith cut in this time, feeling more than a trifle puzzled, 'if you haven't told anyone about Rosemary, which must mean you haven't told anyone where she lives, how on earth did your cousin know where to look?'

'He didn't. Sheer dogged determination, plus a fair smattering of good luck, brought him to your door.'

Leith wasn't so certain about the 'good luck' part of it! She personally could have done without that sort of luck. However, she hid what she was feeling on the subject, and asked the simple question, 'How?'

'Apparently after Naylor had spent hours checking around my old haunts without success, he finally got lucky when someone recalled having many times seen my car parked outside this block of flats. He drove this way and, lo and behold, there was my car. He'd found me.'

See what a bit of dogged determination does for you! Leith thought a tinge acidly, then asked, 'But why should he decide to ring my doorbell?' And, remembering the way the wretched man had kept his finger on the bell, 'He couldn't have been that lucky—to pick on the one flat you were in out of all the others—purely by chance.'

'It wasn't chance, just more good fortune. I don't remember all of last night, although, as I said, bits are coming back all the time. But I think I can take it that I must have been a little—er—unsteady with my actions. At any rate, I must have dropped my car keys quite without knowing it. Naylor entered the building and was still looking for me when there on the mat right outside your door he saw a set of keys which he instantly recognised as mine from the Alsace wine fob on the key-ring.' Travis stood up, his intention to leave clear. 'Thanks for putting me up last night, Leith, and for putting up with me in that condition,' he said sincerely.

'What are friends for?' She smiled as she went with him to the door.

'I'm forgiven, then?'

'Of course,' she assured him cheerfully, but suddenly thought to ask, 'Did you tell your cousin that I wasn't your friend—in the "girlfriend" sense, I mean—by the way?'

'I couldn't. I'm so afraid of slipping up and saying too much. I'm scared to death half the time that when I do start talking about the woman in my life that I won't know where to stop, and. . .' Travis broke off, then asked quickly, 'Naylor—he was all right with you last night?'

'All right?' Leith queried.

'I just thought. . .well, he can be—er—blunt on occasion. If he thought you'd. . .' He broke off, and looked suddenly so exhausted and worn that Leith just didn't have the heart to tell him what an offensive brute his cousin had been.

'He was charming,' she lied, and felt it was worth it to see him look relieved.

By the following morning she had recovered to some

extent from the unusual happenings in her normally well ordered life. Though, oddly, when clad in a shape-concealing full skirt with matching box jacket she drove to work, thoughts of Cousin Naylor, as she had now dubbed him, were still prone to pop into her head.

He was there once more as she turned into the staff car park as again she recalled that 'blunt' hadn't been the word for it! Of course, having spent half the night touring round in the pouring rain searching for Travis wouldn't sweeten anyone's temper, would it, least of all his?

She was happily thinking, Serves him right, a pity there wasn't a cloudburst, when across the car park, in an area where the top managers of Vasey's normally parked their cars, she noticed that room had been made for another car. And what a car! The Jaguar was long, sleek, and up to the minute. Leith was getting out of her short, not so sleek and well past its sell-by date Mini, when she suddenly remembered that Massingham's top brass were moving in that day.

She made her way into the offices and realised that thoughts of Cousin Naylor and his brutishness had wiped from her mind all thought of the Massingham upper echelon's imminent arrival. Though if Jimmy had got it right—and his sources were normally very reliable—and Mr Massingham was indeed going to be one of their number, then she wouldn't be surprised if he had already arrived. That was some smart car out there—and, since they didn't come any more 'top brass' than him, she had the most uncanny feeling that the Jaguar was his.

She said 'Good morning' to several people as she went, and reached her head of department, Robert Drewer's, office, having formed the view that it was no wonder that Massingham's were the go-ahead company they were. It wasn't every head of company who arrived at his place of work before his work-force—the man must be a workaholic!

Leith had a brief discussion with Robert Drewer on a few matters, collected up several files while she was at it, then went to her own office, where her assistant had just arrived.

'Good morning, Jimmy,' she greeted him, and, putting the files down, 'It looks as though we're going to be busy, busy, busy!'

'So what else is new?' he asked cheerfully.

'Would you get me Greatrix on the phone?' she requested. 'Like your tie, by the way!' she commented as she adjusted her horn-rimmed spectacles on the bridge of her nose.

'In honour of our new colleagues,' he grinned. 'You never know, they might look in on us.'

Leith got started on her work, doubting very much that they would so much as catch a glimpse of their new 'colleagues', but she had to smile at his quaint terminology for the higher ranks.

She was proved wrong in her assessment that they would see no one from the new extension, however. For it was around eleven that morning, when she returned to her office after going to consult Dave Smith about some matter, that Jimmy told her chirpily, 'I *knew* I didn't put this tie on for nothing. We've had a visitor!'

'Someone from Massingham's?' Leith queried in surprise.

'None other than the big chief himself!' he revealed.

'Mr Massingham?' she questioned, her surprise showing.

'Cross my heart. He came in with someone from Personnel and Mr Catham,' Jimmy went on, mentioning the name of the manager of Vasey's. 'Mr Catham is apparently introducing him around because Mr Massingham, as well as wanting to meet all heads of department, wanted to see where every departmental office is situated.'

Leith was sorry she'd missed seeing him, but resumed work, realising that since she was only a very small cog in a big machine Mr Massingham would be too busy to make a second visit, or remember, should he be interested in numbers, that there was one member of staff he hadn't met yet.

Half an hour later she was dealing with a small crisis that had cropped up and had forgotten all about Mr Massingham as she sent Jimmy on an urgent trip for some paperwork she needed.

She had her back to the door and was standing at a filing-cabinet taking out more information she would need when she heard her assistant come back. 'Right, Jimmy,' she said, her eyes on the papers in her hand, and was about to add that they'd start with the paperwork he'd collected, when a voice that definitely wasn't Jimmy's cut in.

'Leithia Everett?' questioned an all-masculine voice that didn't belong to any of her fellow workers either— though somehow it seemed to be a voice she'd heard somewhere recently.

Unhurriedly she turned round, her head coming up. Then, for the second time in the short span that she had known the man, her mouth fell open. Shock flooded her as she stared at the tall, dark-haired, dark-eyed man, who seemed in those initial moments not to be believing his eyes either.

'Ye gods!' he grated. 'Not *you*!'

'W-what are you doing here?' she choked, her intelligence trying to tell her something, while with everything she had she didn't want to listen.

She had noticed before that the man whom she'd dubbed Cousin Naylor had a penchant for answering only such queries as he considered he would. He did it again when, leaving her question hanging, he stepped closer, studied her scraped-back hairstyle, then, without so much as a by-your-leave, whipped her glasses from her nose—the better, it seemed, to check that her green eyes were the same green he had looked into during the early hours of Sunday morning. 'My stars, has everybody got *you* wrong!' he rapped insolently, pushing her glasses back at her.

'What's that supposed to mean?' she challenged, hoping her intelligence was wildly wrong, but doubting that it could be.

'How the hell, in the short time you've been here, you've earned the name Miss Frostbite beats me,' he deigned to answer one of her questions, albeit hostilely.

Leith was about to state, quite forcefully, that she was there to work, not to flirt with every male who chanced his arm, when suddenly she realised that if he knew she had worked for Vasey's for only a short while then there was a fair chance either someone from Personnel, or Mr Catham, had given him a brief run-down on each employee before he met them.

'Are you. . .?' she began, but she didn't want to believe what was staring her in the face. 'You're not. . .' she tried again, and could have hit him—a recent tendency—when a mocking look came into his face.

'Oh, I rather think I am,' he drawled, and, just in case she hadn't yet worked it out, though she was certain he knew she had, 'Naylor Massingham,' he introduced himself, and, neither of them offering to shake hands, 'but you can call me "sir".' Like hell she would! 'So,' he went on, his eyes missing nothing, she thought, certainly not the sparks of anger in hers, 'tell me, what's a *nice girl* like you doing in a place like this?' Leith could feel her anger straining at the leash at his sarcastic comment, but she made enormous efforts to stay cool. But on receiving no reply, he seemed hellbent on goading her, and she found she had no chance to be passive, meek and mild, when he went on to taunt, 'You're paid well, I'll grant, but even so. . .' his eyes flicked over her good quality suit which, while not drawing attention to her figure, had been costly '. . . I'd say you'd be hard put to it to pay your expensive dues on that flat you live in.'

'How I pay my mortgage is my own affair!' retorted Leith, well and truly rattled.

'Not when it involves a member of my family!' he snarled, all mockery gone.

'It's got nothing to do with. . .' Leith broke off, suddenly appalled that he must think that his cousin Travis was helping her out with her mortgage repayments.

'It's got everything to do with me!' Naylor Massingham told her harshly. 'You're a bad influence on my cousin,' he stated bluntly. 'He came home plastered again last night.'

'That's not my fault!'

'You're saying that you've not seen him since I half carried him out of your place early yesterday?'

'No, but——'

'I think, Miss Everett,' he cut in before she could tell him that Travis had only called to apologise when he'd stopped by for his car, 'that it might be in your interests not to see him again.'

'In my interests?' she repeated before the penny dropped. 'I. . .' she began. 'You c-can't. . .' she spluttered, trying not to panic that, if she'd got it right—and she couldn't see how else this swine of a man could threaten her—he was saying that her job was on the line! Anger came to her aid then. The *unfairness* of it! 'My private life,' she stood on a matter of principle to declare tartly, 'has nothing *whatsoever* to do with my work!'

Naylor Massingham did not deign to argue. 'You reckon?' he drawled, and walked out.

Leith was sitting stunned, with her glasses still in her hand, when a minute later Jimmy rushed in with the papers he'd been to collect. 'Sorry to be so long—I had to wait for Tom to finish a phone call.' And, his apology out of the way, 'I saw Mr Massingham leaving our office—did I miss anything?'

'With your reputation, Jimmy, I think it unlikely,' she replied lightly, and taking the papers from him, she made a pretence of studying them, but not one fact or figure was she taking in. With a feeling of foreboding she heard again Naylor Massingham's 'You reckon?' She hadn't been as long in this job as her last one, yet she knew there was a positive danger that she might soon be scouring the situations vacant columns again.

She went home that night having had to bring all her professionalism to bear in order to concentrate on the job in hand. Back at her flat, though, she made herself a cup of tea and was able to give her thoughts free rein—all of them centred on Naylor Massingham.

Why hadn't she told him straight out that she was not his cousin's girlfriend? And oh, why hadn't Travis tacked on the surname Massingham when referring to his cousin? Then she would at least have been able to ask if he was anything to do with Massingham Engineering—and thereby have been prepared this morning. She would then, on the vague premise that they might meet, have had her words all sorted and ready, and would have told him that Rosemary, in the flat opposite. . . Suddenly she remembered Travis's horrified 'Lord, *no*!' when she'd suggested that he'd told his mother about Rosemary, and something else struck her. Travis might be going to pieces because he thought Rosemary had finished with him, but, all too clearly, he didn't deep down believe that they were through. Had he been so certain then he wouldn't still be guarding her name so zealously lest any whisper of their attachment got out and so caused Rosemary to decide never to see him again.

Leith went and changed out of her suit and into jeans and a sweater, then took two telephone calls in quick succession—the first from Rosemary.

'Are you all right?' Leith asked quickly, imagining Rosemary to be across the corridor and incapacitated in some way since Rosemary, who always arrived home from work first, invariably popped over if she wanted a chat.

'I'm not back, I'm still in Hazelbury,' Rosemary replied, and explained, 'My mother's unwell, so I've decided to stay on until she's better. I've rung work and told them, and——'

'I'm sorry to hear your mother's poorly. What's wrong with her?' Leith asked, remembering Mrs Green as a woman with a constitution of an ox.

'She's—just—feeling very low,' Rosemary answered. 'Nothing we can quite put our finger on. Anyhow, my father's just taken her to the doctor's, so I thought I'd give you a ring. Not that I couldn't ring you any time while they're here,' she added hurriedly, as if feeling guilty of being underhand while her parents were out of the way.

'Of course,' Leith said quickly. 'Anyhow, you probably waited until I was home to ring me because you know that I work full stretch at the office.' Leith wished she had not, in trying to make Rosemary feel better, mentioned the office. Thoughts of the office conjured up memories of Naylor Massingham—she was very worried about him. 'So how are you?' she forced him out of her mind to ask.

'Fine,' Rosemary replied, but when, unusually, she appeared to have nothing else she wanted to chat about, yet did not ring off, Leith did a swift two-and-two calculation, and the answer she got told her that

Rosemary wanted, in her parents' absence, to talk about Travis.

'I saw Travis over the weekend,' Leith plunged.

'Is he all right?' asked Rosemary, the hint of urgency in her question revealing to Leith that, whatever Rosemary's head was saying, in her heart she still loved Travis very much.

'Quite honestly, Rosemary, he's not so good,' Leith answered, hating to put any pressure on her friend but not knowing how else she could answer.

There was a long long silence, then, 'Look after him for me, Leith,' Rosemary requested, and rang off.

Leith felt saddened by the call. Here were two people clearly in love with each other, hating to be apart from each other and yet with the brick wall of Rosemary's upbringing between them.

She had no time to dwell on the unhappiness of two people of whom she had grown fond, however, for just then her phone rang again. This time it was Travis, a worried Travis, saying that he'd tried to ring Rosemary, but was getting no reply.

'She's always home from work at this time,' he went on. 'Can you——?'

'She's just phoned, actually,' Leith butted in.

'She's all right?'

'She's fine. Her mother's not too well—she's staying on in Hazelbury for a few days,' Leith speedily calmed his fears.

Travis said nothing for a moment, then, 'Did Rosemary—mention me at all?' he wanted to know.

'I told her I'd seen you over the weekend,' she relayed.

'You didn't tell her the state I was in on Saturday night?' he queried, obviously alarmed.

'Of course not!' Leith assured him quickly, and felt dreadfully sorry for him when he clearly sought crumbs of comfort.

'What did she say—about me, I mean?' he asked.

'She asked if you were all right,' Leith replied, not certain that she wasn't breaking confidences, but feeling she would have to be far tougher than she was not to give in to his unspoken plea for some salve on his pain.

'Anything else?' Travis wanted more.

Heck, Leith thought, they loved each other, didn't they? 'Rosemary asked me to look after you,' she let him know.

There was a longer silence from the other end of the phone this time. Then, 'She still loves me, then, despite me being such an idiot as to give her that "see me privately, or not at all" ultimatum?'

'I don't think there was ever any doubt about that,' Leith replied.

'Perhaps not,' Travis agreed, then said how he'd dearly love to ring Rosemary at her parents' home, but that he knew for sure that he could definitely give up even the frail hope he had left of sharing his life with Rosemary if he did that. From then on, as though that had conjured up a bleak picture of him never having a life with his love, he began to sound quite despairing. He spoke of his loneliness of heart and spirit that he wasn't allowed to even talk to his love, and then, as though remembering that Rosemary had asked Leith to look after him, in his loneliness he suddenly asked Leith to have dinner with him. 'If you've got something else on, it's OK,' he added quickly when she did not answer straight away.

The reason that Leith did not immediately answer was that her brain was fully occupied. She rather gathered that what Travis was really asking was if he could come round to her flat and chat a few hours away about Rosemary. It would be no problem for her to make a meal for two, or suggest he bring a take-away, and, prior to this morning, she felt she probably would have agreed

to that. But that morning she had discovered just who
'Cousin Naylor' was, and, even though she was feeling
more than a mite rebellious at his '. . .it might be in
your interests not to see him again', she didn't want to
put her job in jeopardy should Naylor Massingham
happen to be passing, and observe Travis's car again
parked at her apartment block.

'Of course I'll have dinner with you,' she told Travis,
while rebellion was still about her. Even so, though,
since she still didn't want Travis's car outside when he
came to pick her up and bring her back, she added, 'I'll
come in my car—where shall I meet you?'

She got ready to go to the smart hotel which Travis
had named, feeling she could have acted in no other
way. Aside from the fact that she regarded Travis as a
friend too, there was her unspoken promise to Rosemary
that she would look after him to consider. It was true
that Naylor Massingham had apparently said to Travis's
mother that Travis was a big lad now, but Travis was
hurting like the devil inside and was consequently not
handling his unhappiness and loneliness in a very 'big
lad' fashion.

She was driving to meet Travis when something else
Naylor Massingham had said—this time, to her—came
back to her. He'd been full of hostility, she recalled,
when he'd said, 'How the hell, in the short time you've
been here, you've earned the name Miss Frostbite beats
me.' It didn't take long for her to work out how she'd
earned the title. She had still been smarting from her
unjust dismissal for 'over-familiarity with the manage-
ment' at Ardis & Co, when she had wasted no time in
squashing two men in particular at Vasey's who had
shown more interest in her than in their work. Word
must have got around.

Travis, when she met him, looked as dreadful as he
had when he'd called to pick up his car yesterday.

'Thanks for coming,' he greeted her, and escorted her from the foyer of the hotel into the dining-room. From there the head waiter, as if thinking that they were more than friends, escorted them around the bend of the L-shaped room and to a secluded table in a corner.

'What sort of a day have you had?' she asked him lightly, and spent the first course and half of the second in hearing how he didn't think he was giving so much concentration to his job as he should just lately. In no time the conversation drifted naturally to him and Rosemary.

Leith had almost finished her second course when, quite happy to let Travis talk away, she suddenly wondered, as he began to get repetitive, if she was indeed helping him by letting him talk so much on the same theme. She decided to change the subject.

'I never told you!' she exclaimed suddenly, then added, 'Well, you already know, I expect—but I didn't.' And when he looked at her in mystification, as well he might, she realised, she went on, 'I'd no idea until this morning that the same Naylor who came for you yesterday morning is my new boss!'

'Really?' Travis queried, and, for the first time in an age, he smiled as he tacked on, 'Now that you mention it, I seem to remember now reading something about Massingham's taking over Vasey's, but Naylor's always got his finger in some negotiation, so the Vasey deal would have gone out of my head while I read about his next business venture.'

'He doesn't talk about his achievements, then?'

'He might discuss some business matters with my father, for whom he has a tremendous respect, but apart from the fact that he doesn't live at Parkwood any more he never boasts.' Very commendable, I'm sure, Leith, having no liking for Naylor Massingham, was thinking

sourly when suddenly, as if thinking over their conversation of a minute ago, Travis started to look alarmed. 'I
say,' he broke into hurried speech, 'you won't say
anything to Naylor about Rosemary and me, will you?'
And before Leith could say a word to lessen his agitation,
'Heaven alone knows what chance I've got with
Rosemary *now*, but she'd finish with me for sure, I know
she would, if anyone else knew about us!'

'I know Rosemary feels eaten up by guilt that she's
fallen in love with you while she's married to someone
else, but surely——' Leith tried to reason.

'Promise you won't tell him,' Travis interrupted, and
Leith knew then that she could talk to him until she was
blue in the face, but he was just not hearing.

'I probably won't see him again,' she muttered hopefully, but, because Travis was not satisfied, but sat
tensely waiting, 'I—promise,' she agreed.

Instantly the tension went from him. 'Thanks, Leith,'
he said quietly, and added emotionally, 'Lord, I always
thought that being in love would be a wonderful time!
Want to know something?—it's murder!' He swallowed,
then, as she had done earlier, opted to find a different
topic. 'Have you heard from Sebastian recently?' he
enquired.

Talk of Sebastian, but not the financial problem he
had left Leith with, occupied the remainder of the time
until they had finished their meal. 'That was a super
dinner,' Leith thanked Travis as she put down her
coffee-cup, ready to go.

'Glad you enjoyed it,' he commented, calling the
waiter over so he could settle the bill.

Leith gathered up her bag, her thoughts already on
getting home and trying to get a full eight hours' sleep
so as to be sharp for work in the morning.

As soon as Travis got to his feet, she was beside him.
He was close behind her as they rounded the L-bend of

the restaurant—and he very nearly cannoned into her when she suddenly stopped dead. Having driven herself to meet Travis to obviate Naylor Massingham knowing that she hadn't heeded his '. . .in your interests not to see him again' warning, Leith discovered that she need not have bothered. Naylor Massingham knew anyway. For there, dining with a beautiful blonde, was none other than Naylor himself—and—he was looking nowhere but at Leith!

She saw his glance flick to Travis, who stepped to the side of her when she halted, then Travis too saw Naylor. Though, in Travis's case, instead of being horror-struck, he seemed genuinely pleased to see his cousin.

'Naylor!' He went forward, taking hold of Leith's arm so that, there being nothing other she could do if she wanted to keep her dignity, she had to go forward too.

The boss of Massingham's had superb manners in company, Leith had to give him that, for as they reached his table he rose to his feet. She saw his eyes flick over her neatly fitting cotton lace blouse and down to her hip-hugging velvet culottes. Nervously her hand went up to adjust her glasses—then she remembered that she wasn't wearing glasses, and as his glance moved to her loose-flowing and luxuriant shining chestnut hair she felt decidedly vulnerable.

'You know Leith, of course.' Travis, when she would rather he hadn't, was equally well mannered and had decided introductions were in order. 'Leith's just been telling me that you both work for the same firm,' he put on a front for the rest of the world to joke.

'How are you, Leith?' Naylor Massingham enquired, but while his handsomely defined mouth moved in a pleasant upward curve, the hard-as-flint eyes that pierced her large green-eyed look told a very different story.

'Fine, thanks,' she murmured, but as he turned to introduce his companion, Olinda Bray, she was shaking inside. Travis had raised himself out of his despair to quip that she and his cousin both worked for the same firm, but the message that had come across to her from the dark steely look of Naylor Massingham was that that might be true now, but, since she had chosen not to heed his warning, one of them would not be working for the same firm for very much longer!

CHAPTER THREE

LEITH wondered, as she drove to work the next morning, why she had bothered getting the car out, since she was convinced that, his warning unheeded, Naylor Massingham would waste no time in getting her out of his business.

She parked her car with the ever-present worry about her mortgage on her mind and was, in a weak moment, of the opinion that she should try to get through to Naylor Massingham that she was not his cousin's girl-friend, and to explain the innocence of Travis staying the night at her flat. Would he let her, though? She remembered the glint of steel in his eyes last night, and she knew then that she would be lucky if he allowed her to get that far into explaining anything. Damning her weakness, as rebellion started to stir, she damned her circumstances too that had provoked that weakness. Far from being tempted to explain anything then, she was of the view that she'd see him in hell first. Who did he think he was anyway, that he could push her around?

'Morning, Jimmy,' she greeted her assistant as she went into her office, and, of the mind that, until she heard differently, she still had a job, 'let's get down to it!'

Despite her mutinous feelings, though, the first couple of hours passed with Leith on tenterhooks each time the phone rang or the door opened. Would he do the deed himself, or get Personnel to do it? Somehow, and she didn't know why, she couldn't see him getting anybody else to do his dirty work.

When midday arrived and she still had her job at

Vasey's, Leith began to have doubts that Naylor Massingham intended to dismiss her. At one o'clock she went to lunch feeling more confident about her long-term prospects with the firm. What reason could he give for dismissing her anyway? There was nothing whatsoever the matter with her work!

She returned from lunch at ten to two in a happier frame of mind. At two o'clock precisely the phone rang; Jimmy answered it. 'It's for you,' he said, holding his hand over the mouthpiece. 'It's a Miss Russell.'

The name meant nothing to her. 'Miss Russell?' she queried as she stretched out a hand to the phone.

For a moment, as he screwed up his face in concentration, she thought her knowledgeable assistant was going to let her down. Then, 'The only one I can think of is a Miss Moira Russell, Mr Massingham's secretary.'

'Thanks,' Leith smiled. If her happier frame of mind had just hit the floor with a crash, she was the only person who was going to know it. 'Leith Everett,' she stated down the phone, and soon knew she had been living in a fool's paradise these last few hours.

'Oh, hello, Miss Everett,' Moira Russell greeted her congenially. 'I'm Mr Massingham's secretary,' she introduced herself in case Leith should be wondering who she was. 'Mr Massingham would like to see you——'

'Now?' Leith, while her voice stayed calm, jumped the gun.

'He has a busy afternoon. If you could be sure to make yourself available, I'll give you a ring when we can slot you in,' the efficient woman said pleasantly.

Leith did not bother asking what Mr Massingham wanted to see her about—she had no need to. She knew quite well why she would be trotting over to the new extension when summoned.

'Thank you, I'll do that,' she replied with equal pleasantness, and put the phone down to rebel angrily that the diabolical swine, when he'd got no reason to dismiss her, was about to do just that.

Why she stayed on waiting for that phone call Leith couldn't have said, though she thought her very large concern about paying her mortgage had something to do with it. Perhaps she should stay and try and make out a case for herself. What sort of case had she got, though? she thought hopelessly. Maybe, then, it was stubborn pride that was making her stay waiting for Moira Russell to telephone again. Pride that demanded she ask Naylor Massingham for a better reason for sacking her than the fact that his cousin was making himself ill over her.

Leith's mutiny ebbed when she thought how ill and distraught Travis was making himself over his love, and the seed of an idea of appealing to Travis to save her job withered before it was half born. Travis had enough on his plate just now without being asked to go against his promise to Rosemary to reveal nothing about her. For it was certain, Leith considered, that with the evidence Naylor Massingham had of seeing Travis in bed at her flat, and again seeing her with Travis in that hotel dining-room, he was going to want more from Travis than any declaration of, 'Leith isn't my girlfriend, so don't sack her'.

Three o'clock came, then four, and still Leith hadn't received the summons she was starting to get really uptight about. When five o'clock came and Jimmy began to tidy his desk, she was not thinking at all kindly about her employer.

'Are you staying on, Leith?' asked Jimmy, aware by then that she was not a clock-watcher, and sometimes stayed behind to finish something.

'I won't be long after you,' she told him lightly.

'Do you want me to stay too?'

'You go.' She smiled her thanks for his willing offer. 'I can manage this on my own.'

Could she? Leith wondered when he'd gone. She liked her job, she needed her job, the building society with whom she had her mortgage would very much like her to keep her well-paying job—but she had no idea how she could go about keeping it if that swine in the new extension said, 'On your way'.

By six o'clock, when even the tail-enders of the department had gone, Leith had swung from wanting with everything she had to hang on to her job, to be furious enough with the man who was making her sweat it out to tell him exactly what he could do with it.

She wouldn't do that, however—she knew that ten minutes later when still no call had come. Not that she would grovel either—devil take it, she'd keep some pride! But she'd be as cool and calm as she could as she tried to point out to Naylor Massingham the unfairness of his action.

So she thought then, but, when another fifteen minutes went by and her phone stayed silent, rebellion once more bombarded the cool and calm front she was trying to erect. Just *who* did he think he was, leaving her there to squirm? She'd be damned if she'd squirm! Like *hell* she'd squirm!

A moment later Leith had her phone in her hand. A swift check of internal numbers, and, half expecting Moira Russell to have left ages ago, she was ringing her number.

'Mr Massingham's secretary,' Moira answered clearly, and Leith realised that, like her employer, she was no doubt working late.

'Leithia Everett here,' Leith announced formally, and without pausing to let the secretary get a word in, had she been going to, 'Would you give Mr Massingham my apologies, please? I have to go now—I've an important engagement.'

Why she had tacked that last bit on, Leith found it

difficult to know as she made her way to the car park.
Quite possibly because whatever she personally felt about
Naylor Massingham, manners were still manners. And
to a third party—in this case Moira Russell—it would
sound better to offer an excuse than to add, 'so tell him
to put that in his drum and bang it'.

Leith was reversing her car when she spotted the
Jaguar which she had first seen—grief, was it only
yesterday morning? If it was his, and she felt certain that
it was, then he was still working, still hard at it. Good!
That should keep him away from Olinda Bray!

Good heavens! What on earth had brought that on?
Leith wondered. As if she cared a damn about his social
life—or however many luscious blondes he went out
with!

Leith wasn't feeling very hungry when she got in, but
she made herself a pot of tea and a snack, and, as she
realised she had known she would, she worried. Not that
she regretted her action in coming home when she had—
she'd waited all afternoon, for goodness' sake, and then
some.

Starting to feel a little frazzled round the edges, she
went and had a bath, donned a nightdress and cotton
wrap, and brushed out her hair. It was too early to go to
bed yet—though she'd an idea that while this worry was
on her mind she wouldn't be doing a lot of sleeping.

She was not feeling in her sunniest humour as she
wondered if she was going to have to wait all day
tomorrow for her summons, when someone rang her
doorbell. On answering it, with a sick feeling in the pit
of her stomach, she realised she wasn't going to have to
wait until tomorrow to receive her marching orders.

Though, to start with, her initial feeling was one of
total shock as she pulled back her door and saw Naylor
Massingham standing there. Indeed, so shaken was she
that, without being fully aware of what she was doing,

she had invited him in and had led the way into her sitting-room before she had got herself back together again. Then it was that, with him towering over her, she took a step back and observed that Naylor Massingham must have some highly confidential papers in his brief-case since, evidently not trusting to leave it in his car, he had chosen to bring it up to her flat with him.

She saw his glance rake her from the top of her shining chestnut hair over her make-up-free face, and down over her pretty cotton wrap to the tips of her toes. She had been nearly speechless from seeing him so unexpectedly, and was a mass of agitation inside at what he was about to say. But both speechlessness and agitation went flying when, eyeing her sardonically, he did open his mouth.

'All dressed ready for your important engagement, I see,' he drawled, his eyes going once more over her bedroom attire, and, if that wasn't enough to ignite sparks of fury in her, his mocking tone abruptly fell away as his glance went from her and to the hall—in which direction she knew he was aware there was at least one bedroom. 'Or do you have a guest here already?' he snarled.

'No, I don't!' Leith erupted, and hated Naylor Massingham with all that was in her—him *and* his offensive questions!

With flashing eyes she stared hostilely up at him. Entirely unmoved, he looked down into her large and angry green eyes. Then, seemingly not in any hurry to state his business and be away, he put his briefcase down and queried, 'But you are expecting someone tonight?'

Leith took a deep and controlling breath, then took the fight—for that was how she regarded it—into his camp. 'I'm not seeing Travis tonight, if that's what you're asking,' she told him coolly.

'Oh, I know that,' he condescended to state. 'He went abroad on his father's business this morning.'

'Trying to trip me up?' queried Leith, giving no inkling that this was news to her. Travis hadn't said anything about going abroad last night. She saw Naylor Massingham's hand in this somewhere. Travis had said that his father was respected by his cousin. Was it a two-way respect—had the two got their heads together and decided it might be beneficial to Travis to send him out of the country for a short while?

She had no time to dwell on the matter, however, because, ever a man with no time for prevarication, he replied, 'Not trying to trip you up at all,' then grated bluntly, 'More trying to discover just how many "close" men friends you do have.' Leith was still blinking at him and his nerve when he went on, 'I know you wear a "hands off" sign at the office. . .' well, that was something, she supposed '. . .but how long have you been wearing a deerstalker?'

'Deer. . .' She broke off, quickly realising that here was a man who missed nothing. From where they were standing there was no way he could see the hat-and-coat fitment, yet he knew, and had taken a full inventory of its contents. 'The deerstalker's not mine,' she told him.

'Surprise me?' he grunted.

Leith gave him a speaking look. 'If you must know, it's a hat Sebastian left behind w——' she began, and was rudely chopped off when Naylor Massingham went back to being a snarling brute again.

'So, for all you were so thick with Travis last night, my cousin's not your only lover!'

'*Lover*!' Leith exclaimed, and was so startled, by both his words and his attack, that she had no chance to cover how startled she felt.

'My oath—so innocent!' Naylor Massingham grated. Then suddenly a demoniacal light had entered his eyes and, since he seemed to be a man who would set about proving his own theories—in this case that it was inconceivable that she should be as innocent as she would appear—he took a couple of steps forward and reached for her.

Leith had never been kissed like it. While it was true that because working hard for qualifications left small time—or inclination either, she had to admit—to indulge in such pastimes, she had been kissed before; never like this! Even while, at first, she fought like fury in his arms, she realised his intent. But his arms were strong, like iron bands around her, and there was no breaking the insistence of his hold, nor any breaking away from the closeness of his body. Nor, she soon discovered, was there any avoiding of his pursuing, determined mouth.

'No!' she managed to gasp, succeeding briefly in freeing her mouth from his.

It was all she was capable of saying for quite some time, for he had captured her lips again and was kissing her with a deeper intensity. She felt him draw her closer up against his body—and suddenly a tingling sensation started somewhere inside her. She attempted to push him away, and then, as his wonderful mouth gentled over hers, she knew that to push him away was not what she wanted either.

His hands caressed her back, then caressed down to her waist, and when they reached her hips he moulded her thinly clad body against him. 'Oh,' she gasped, and, as flames of wanting started to flicker into life, her arms went up and around him, and she freely gave him her lips.

She was in a mindless world where she had forgotten everything about why he was there, mindless that not half an hour ago she had thought him the most hateful of men when, abruptly, shatteringly, he suddenly stilled.

In the next second, he had pushed her away from him! Left staring at him while waiting for her full wits to return, Leith did not know for the moment what on earth was going on. It did not take Naylor Massingham to tell her.

She was still rocking from the unexpected power his kisses had over her when, looking down at her from his lofty height, he mocked, 'Now try and tell me you aren't just anybody's!'

What he had just said hit her like a douche of cold water, and instantly Leith, while wanting to hammer the living daylights out of him, —although still forgetful of her tenuous job position—was otherwise working on full brain power.

'So why,' she fired hotly, 'if it wasn't to prove how devastatingly attractive to women you are, have you come here?' She was seething, and was not certain, as she fought for control, that she wouldn't physically lash out at him yet. Then she had the severest strain put on the control of her newly awakened ear-boxing predilection when his mouth twitched at the corners and it seemed, for a moment, that her sarcasm had amused him.

She was soon left in no doubt at all, however, that she was very much mistaken. For Naylor Massingham looked far from amused, and was in fact glowering at her darkly as he rapped toughly, 'The purpose of my wanting to see you, Miss Everett, was to give you verbal warning that unless your work improves you're *out*!'

'Out?' she exclaimed, up in arms at once that, when she knew she did a jolly good job, he should try to make out that she didn't. 'What's wrong with my work?' she challenged him spiritedly.

He did not answer straight away but stared, quite unruffled, down into her angry green eyes. Then, with a mocking look which she was beginning to detest as much as she detested him, he asked softly, 'Ever hear of the Norwood & Chambers contract?'

'That's not fair!' Leith exploded. 'The Norwood & Chambers contract was started long before I joined the company. I only——'

'Finished it,' he concluded for her, and Leith knew then that if Naylor Massingham had been looking to find fault with her work then plainly he'd left no stone unturned.

'But I can't be held responsible for——' she tried to argue—and got shot down in flames for her trouble.

'One of the first rules an executive in your salary grade has to accept,' he sliced her off, 'is that when the flak starts flying you take responsibility for what comes out of your office whether your signature's on the work or not!' And, having given her a lecture she didn't need, 'We made a loss on the Norwood & Chambers transaction,' he told her. Then pleasantly—too pleasantly—he added, 'End your relationship with Travis, and I might be prepared to forget about it.'

'That's blackmail!' Leith accused angrily, and saw at once that he didn't appear to take too kindly to her accusation.

'Call it what the hell you like!' he rapped, and she knew that was the way it was going to be.

Needing a moment's breathing-space, she took a side-step or two away, and had a brief inner tussle where she came close to telling him that Travis was not her boyfriend, and had never been her boyfriend. Then she flicked a glance to Naylor Massingham and knew at once, from his tough, belligerent stance, that he was never going to believe her. Not unless she told him all about Rosemary who lived opposite, anyhow.

A moment later Leith took a grip on herself. For heaven's sake, she was fond of Rosemary and Travis, and regarded both of them as friends, yet here she was almost about to betray them. Good grief, she was being quite pathetic!

Her intelligence was working overtime when next she

looked at her employer. And she was glad to have the
strength of anger against him as she deciphered coolly,
'What you're really saying is that either I leave Travis
alone, or, if you can't get me over the Norwood &
Chambers contract, you won't rest until you find some
other contract I've had small dealings with and which
didn't work out, which added together will amount to
dereliction of duty.'

She really did detest his mockery, for it was there
again as he drawled, 'Brainy as well as beautiful!' Then,
while Leith was again holding down the urge to hit him,
and seeing that he'd prefer not to sack her without just
cause—thereby deeply offending his cousin—he had
bent and picked up his briefcase.

With more than a touch of relief, she thought he was
about to go. But no, what he actually did was to open up
his briefcase and extract a file from it. Without a word,
he handed the file to her. She opened it, scrutinised the
first of the many pages it contained, then took her eyes
from it to query, 'Palmer & Pearson? I don't
normally. . .'

'You do now,' he told her authoritatively. 'Work on
that,' he instructed, and added loftily, 'That should keep
you out of mischief for a while.'

With that, just as if he thought he had wasted more
than enough time with her, he went, and Leith was left
staring mutinously after him. She had enough to do
without him coming and bringing her what she could
tell, from the little she'd read so far, was some very
important work.

She found it impossible to settle after his visit, and
spent the time until she went to bed silently reviling
him. Him and his verbal warnings! In the normal run of
things, had a verbal warning been necessary—which it
certainly wasn't—then it was without question that
Naylor Massingham would certainly not have wasted his

precious time on such trips, but would have delegated one of his underlings to do it.

When she later climbed into bed, though, she was human enough to have found—out of all the unpleasantness that had gone on—a couple of things of a complimentary nature. The one, that, even while giving her a verbal warning about her work, he had handed her a very important file to work on—albeit only to ensure she had little time for anything else—must mean that he had received good reports on her ability. The other, even though it was certain that he hadn't meant it as a compliment, was his 'Brainy as well as beautiful!' comment.

She closed her eyes and was uncertain what soothed the effects of his brutishness most—the fact that he thought her good enough to tackle the Palmer & Pearson work, the fact that he thought her brainy, or the fact that he thought her beautiful. Strangely, her last waking thoughts centred on none of them, nor even his blackmailing threat to her job over Travis. What haunted her was the way he had kissed her—and how she had been unable to do anything but respond!

By Friday Leith had pushed all memory of Naylor Massingham's kisses to the back of her mind. She had other, more important things to think about, for goodness' sake. She was feeling decidedly piggy-in-the-middle in more ways than one. Rosemary had not returned from her parents' home yet; Travis was either still abroad or was coping better, for he had not contacted her again. But if things were quiet on the Rosemary and Travis front, Leith was very much aware that there was a brute of a man in the new extension who was only biding his time before he tripped her up.

Which was why she was checking and double-checking everything that landed on her desk. As well as coping with that, she was also having to include some thorough and painstaking work on the Palmer & Pearson file which Naylor Massingham had handed her on Tuesday evening. Since she had been working more or less at full stretch before she'd been given the extra work to do, there was only one way she could fit more work into her day, and that was by working late at the office, then going home with a bulging briefcase.

She went to work on Friday morning having worked until midnight the night before, and giving serious consideration to finding another job. Vasey's were not the be-all and end-all, she decided, then realised that, with not another word coming from her brother Sebastian, not so much as another postcard, much less a banker's draft with his share of the mortgage, they were the only firm around that paid the sort of money she was earning.

What she could have done without when she went into her office was to answer the phone and hear Jimmy Webb ring in to ask if she could do without him as he'd got an upset stomach. For upset stomach read hangover, she thought, knowing he'd been to an eighteenth birthday celebration for one of his friends the night before.

But he was a most willing worker, and although she knew she was in for a tough day without him she offered her sympathy, and advised, 'Take an Alka-Seltzer and go back to bed. I'll see you on Monday.' She then, in between coping with phone calls, half of which Jimmy would normally have handled, got on with what she was paid to do.

By early afternoon Leith owned that she was feeling more than a little drained. It was about two-thirty, however, when she had need to go for a file which Jimmy would, had he been there, have fetched for her in no time. Come back, Jimmy, all is forgiven, she thought with a trace of humour, as, leaving her office, she went on the errand herself.

But, trace of humour or not, she was in no mood for

the antics of Paul Fisher, one of the men who worked in the same department, who, regardless of her repressive glasses and old-maid hairstyle, was forever ready to make advances. They both entered a corridor at the same time, she going one way, he the other. She saw him coming and intended to give him a wide berth. He, on seeing her, had, it appeared, other ideas. For there was absolutely no need at all for him to walk so close to where she was walking or to bump into her and so catch her off balance—the end result being that he had his arms around her, as if to save her, before she could stop him.

Though she did stop him before he could get further than to spin her round and begin in a supposed-to-be-seductive tone, 'If you want the thrill of a lifetime, Leith——'

'Take your hands off me!' Leith snapped, feeling sick inside as a revolting memory of Alec Ardis hit her. 'When I'm *that* hard up that I'd welcome your attentions, you pea-brained slug, I'll let you know! Meanwhile,' she pushed forcefully at him, uncaring that they might have an audience, when his glance shot over her shoulder, 'keep your licentious grubby paws to yourself!'

That he let her go, and that she was free of him so easily was a great relief, but she was shaken from the unwanted experience, and as he swiftly went on his way she turned round—but only to collide with someone else.

This really isn't my day, she thought when, as she pushed at whoever it was, she was again caught off balance. The hands that caught hold of her this time, though, did not pass beyond the bounds of normal assistance. Abruptly she looked up—straight into the night-black eyes of Naylor Massingham.

For long seconds, his expression serious, he looked

down into her large green eyes, then, 'You're trembling!' he observed.

For a few moments Leith felt transfixed—there seemed to be a hint of kindness in his look. Then his glance flicked down to her mouth, lingered there for a moment—and she just knew that he was remembering those kisses they had shared.

Abruptly she pulled out of his hold. 'Men!' she snapped angrily.

His hands at once fell from her arms, and the only kindness in his glance, she realised quickly, had been in her imagination. For there was nothing but mockery there as he scorned loftily, 'Don't tell me you've taken the cure?' Leith put her head in the air, took a side-step, and marched on her way.

Deciding she'd had enough of her office for that week, she filled her briefcase to bulging with work she could do at home, and closed her office door at five sharp. She was just walking from the building when she saw Paul Fisher.

Feeling more than ready to pass him without acknowledgement, she found, however, that he wasn't of the same mind. 'Thanks!' he commented petulantly.

'What for?' she enquired coldly, not faltering in her step.

'Miss Butter-wouldn't-melt! Thanks to you, I've just had a lecture from old man Drewer—his theme being my long-term employment with this company in relation to sexual harassment.'

'Couldn't happen to a nicer guy!' Leith hid her surprise to tell him sharply, and walked away from him to where she had parked her car.

Quite clearly, Paul Fisher thought she had reported him to his superior, but she knew full well that she hadn't. Still, she didn't mind at all having the blame laid at her door if it saved some other female from having to put up with his unwanted attentions. Somebody must have reported him, though, mustn't they?

Her glance flew to the Jaguar, parked where it was always parked these days, and a hint of a smile warmed her mouth. Hadn't Naylor Massingham been the only other person around at the time of that incident?

She got into her car and pointed it homewards, and, unable to see who else but he would have contacted Paul Fisher's head of department, she unexpectedly started to feel quite kindly disposed to Naylor Massingham.

She wondered how much he had witnessed, then realised he must have seen, and heard, most of it to order Paul Fisher to be carpeted, without suggesting Mr Drewer get her side of it.

She suddenly became aware that she must have been thinking of Naylor Massingham for quite a bit of the journey, when she was all at once incredibly jolted by a question that flashed into her head out of nowhere. She had felt quite revolted when Alec Ardis had, without the smallest encouragement, grabbed her; she had felt nauseated when Fisher had, uninvited, caught hold of her; so why had she felt none of these things last Tuesday night, when Naylor Massingham had taken her in his arms?

CHAPTER FOUR

THE answer to why she had felt neither violent revulsion nor nausea when she had been in Naylor Massingham's arms evaded Leith. But, she decided, when she got up on Saturday morning, she had better things to do than to let such matters worry her. With a stuffed-to-capacity briefcase, she had better things to do with her time too, anyway.

After her breakfast, she did her usual Saturday chores, then opened up the dining-room table to its full extent, and, placing everything in neat individual sections, emptied her briefcase. Then her mother rang.

'Have you heard from Sebastian?' was her mother's first excited question.

'I can tell *you* have.' Leith smiled.

'I had a letter this morning, a lovely long one. He's met such a nice girl!'

Sebastian sometimes did. 'Is he coming home?' Leith crossed her fingers and hoped.

'Not for ages; I shouldn't think we'll see him this side of Christmas,' her mother cheerfully squashed Leith's hopes—Christmas was seven months away! 'He and Elise are travelling around India and after they've been everywhere there they plan to go on to Thailand and. . .' Leith blanked off for a moment as, with sinking spirits, she felt it would be a wonder if Sebastian found himself free to return to pay something off his mortgage the Christmas after next, let alone this coming one. '. . .it's a wonderful opportunity.'

'It certainly is.' Leith mentally shook herself to join in the conversation, realising that her mother had been speaking of the wonderful opportunities there were for world-wide travelling these days. 'I suppose he's written to his firm telling them not to keep his job open for him?' Sebastian's 'holiday' had been meant to be of a fortnight's duration only.

'Oh, I expect so, dear,' her mother replied, quite obviously thrilled at the lovely long letter she had received from her adored son.

'Did he—er—mention what he's going to do for money while he's away?' Leith asked, unable in her constant nagging worry about the mortgage to resist the hope that he might have referred to it, and given some indication of what he intended to do about repaying his half.

'Well, he—er. . .' her mother replied uncomfortably, and Leith forgot her own hopes to feel quite cross with her brother.

'He's never written asking you to send him some money?'

'Why shouldn't he?' asked Mrs Everett, sounding quite sharp in his defence. 'Sending his mortgage money every month must be difficult for him!' Leith knew she'd be to blame somewhere. 'And, as he said in his letter, it was all right for him to rough it a little while he was on his own, but he has Elise to think of now.'

And naturally Elise hasn't any money to pay her own way, Leith thought, but, since she didn't want to part bad friends with her mother, she managed to hold back. 'What does Dad think?' she asked instead.

'Er—he's out playing golf,' her mother replied, and, while Leith was beginning to wonder how long it would be before her father discovered that his joint savings account with his wife had a dent in it, her mother was swiftly changing the subject. 'How about you, Leith, do you have any small problem you need help with?'

'I'm fine. Not a problem in the world.' Leith, with

two very large problems staring her in the face—the mortgage and Naylor Massingham, despite his action yesterday still there metaphorically breathing down her neck—thought a denial preferable to dampening her mother's present happy frame of mind.

'You were always such a capable child,' Mrs Everett replied cheerfully, having absolutely no idea, Leith knew, of the times she'd kept childhood and then adolescent worries to herself on account of Sebastian's suffering either catastrophe or crisis at the same time. 'By the way,' her mother went on, 'you never told me that Rosemary Green had left her husband!'

Leith was momentarily taken aback. Her village, like any other, had its share of gossipmongers who took the sketchiest rumour and added and added to it. But Rosemary would hate it if word had got out, and was going around, that she and her husband had split up.

Leith fought a dreadful battle with her conscience when her friendship with Rosemary vied with the necessity of telling her mother an outright lie. 'Rosemary hasn't left her husband.' She spoke only the truth.

She might well have owned that it was the other way round and that Rosemary's husband had been the one to do the leaving, Leith realised, when her mother retorted, 'Well, she's not living at her flat, is she? She's back home!'

'Her mother's not well.'

'She looked well enough to me when I saw her on the cake section of the WI stall yesterday morning!'

There was nothing for it. 'I never knew you were such a gossip, Mother,' Leith teased.

'I'm not!' her mother denied. 'I only. . .'

Always glad to speak to her parent, Leith came away from the phone half wishing just the same that her mother had not rung. As well as giving her cause to be anxious about Rosemary—whose parents would make life most uncomfortable for her if the rumours circulating the village ever reached them—it was a blow to know that Sebastian would be away for the rest of the year.

Writing to him would do no good, she knew that before that idea could land. By the sound of it he intended to move around anyway, so it was doubtful that any letter she wrote would reach him. And anyhow, with Sebastian writing to their mother for money, it was a foregone conclusion that he would have none left over with which to honour his responsibilities.

Leith spent the next few minutes in accepting that somehow she was going to have to pay her brother's share of the hefty monthly repayment as well as her own for the next seven months minimum. Now how in creation was she going to find that sort of money? If she lived frugally, penurised herself, she could cope with one month, possibly two, but after that. . .

She went over to the dining table and, in the hope of drowning her worries in work, sat down. It was then, though, that she realised that, having wanted to come to London, having made the break from Hazelbury—as lovely as Hazelbury was—she did not want to return there unless it was absolutely necessary. She enjoyed living in London, she more than enjoyed the work she did, and she wanted to stay. When, out of nowhere, a picture of Naylor Massingham suddenly presented itself, Leith reached for the nearest folder. Now why? She liked London, she liked her job, but——Suddenly she wasn't so sure about him.

She was deep into her work that afternoon when Rosemary rang. 'When are you coming back?' Leith asked promptly, sometimes not seeing Rosemary for days, but missing her now she wasn't around.

'Not yet. My parents are being a bit stuffy about me living in London on my own, actually,' Rosemary confessed. And while Leith was thinking, heavens,

Rosemary was a year older than her and had been married, and was starting to feel grateful that she had the parents she had, Rosemary was going on, 'They're both out at the moment.' There was a brief pause, then Rosemary was rushing on as if fearful that they would be back before she had said what she'd rung up to say, which was, 'Can I ask a favour, Leith?'

In Leith's view, Rosemary and her unhappy conscience were way overdue for a favour. 'Anything,' she said willingly.

'The thing is, Travis has just phoned——'

'Travis?'

'Yes—from Italy,' Rosemary replied, and Leith could clearly hear a smile in her friend's voice as though it had cheered her so much to hear Travis. That smile had gone, though, when Rosemary went on, 'Fortunately, my parents weren't in—I just don't know what I'd have done had they been here. The thing is, I was lucky this time, but I've had to tell Travis that he must never ring me here again.'

'But you do still love him?' Leith questioned tentatively.

There was a brief pause, then, 'So very much,' Rosemary said softly. 'But my parents are very upset that, regardless of the fact that my marriage ended up being so awful, I'm not making any effort to get back with Derek.'

'Haven't you told them he's living with someone else?'

'I have, but it makes no difference—they'd be furious if they knew about Travis. Which is why I'm ringing,' Rosemary revealed, and confessed, 'I haven't let myself face how lonely I was for the sound of his voice. It was marvellous when he rang, but since I can't have him ringing here again, I told him, in a moment of my feelings getting the better of me, that if he does have any message for me he could contact you, and you'd pass it on. Would you?' Rosemary asked.

'Of course!' Leith agreed without hesitation, and only later realised that after that promise there was no way now she could, as Naylor Massingham decreed, 'finish' with Travis. She did not doubt that Travis would soon be in touch.

He was. Though it was Sunday evening and he was still in Italy. 'Leith, it's me—Travis.' she heard when she picked up the phone.

'So how's Travis?' she asked lightly.

'I've spoken to Rosemary.'

'I know—she rang me.'

'Did she? The darling! She's asked you about our—arrangement, then?'

'It'll be a pleasure,' Leith assured him. 'Do you have any message?' she asked, in her 'go-between' capacity.

'Only to tell her I love her—though she knows that,' he replied. 'You needn't ring her especially, or her parents will think it peculiar if you ring every day to tell her that from me. She's forgiven me for being such an ass with my ultimatum the other day,' he added, then sighed, 'I do wish she was coming back to her flat.'

'When are you returning to England, by the way?' Leith asked quickly as she sensed he was getting a bit down.

'My father's given me tons of work, but I'm in front of target,' he replied, and sounded a little more cheerful.

Leith went to her office on Monday, having spent more of the weekend working on facts and figures, yet finding she was glad it was Monday morning. 'You're better?' she greeted Jimmy.

'Never again!' he vowed, looking slightly shamefaced. 'It took me until yesterday to fully open my eyes.' Leith laughed.

She was not laughing ten minutes later when, just as

she had sent Jimmy on an errand, the phone rang and she answered it. 'Moira Russell here,' the top-grade secretary announced herself. 'Mr Massingham would like to see you straight away, if it's convenient.'

'Very well,' Leith replied, knowing that she wouldn't at all have liked the answer had she queried, what if it isn't convenient? 'Mr Massingham would like to see you straight away' was an order.

'Here you are, Leith.' Her assistant breezed in with some figures she wanted, just as she was taking hold of the Palmer & Pearson file.

'Leave them on my desk, Jimmy,' she bade him, and, because it wasn't efficient not to tell him where she would be if needed, 'Mr Massingham wants to see me. I—er—shouldn't be long.' She left her office with the uncomfortable feeling that Jimmy, who missed nothing, had noticed that she was looking a little flushed.

She made for the new extension, hoping she had imagined that speculative look in her young assistant's eye, and feeling that she'd better let him think the Palmer & Pearson file had dropped on her desk while he was absent on Friday. It would never do for him to know that Mr Massingham had brought the file to her home personally. Despite her assistant's undoubted loyalty to her, that titbit would be just too much for the miss-nothing Jimmy to keep to himself.

Leith reached the new extension and owned that she was feeling churned up inside. That did not surprise her. Naylor Massingham had not been the easiest of people to deal with when he'd been in her home; how would she fare now that she was, so to speak, on his territory?

Asking directions as she went, she entered what she realised was Moira Russell's office, when a woman in her early thirties, slim and immaculate, raised her head from what she was doing and enquired pleasantly, 'Miss Everett?'

Civilities cost nothing. 'Good morning,' Leith smiled.
'I believe Mr Massingham wanted to see me.'

'If you'd like to take a seat for a moment.' Moira
Russell returned her smile, and went to another door in
the room, where she tapped and went in. Here we go,
Leith thought, fully expecting to be still sitting there at
midday. Pleasingly, however, though to energise her
heart into a few racing beats, Moira Russell came out
almost immediately and, holding the door she had just
come through open, smiled and said, 'Mr Massingham
will see you now.'

Leith smiled in return and, leaving her seat, went over
to the door. She managed to keep her smile in place too
as she walked into the thickly carpeted room and closed
the door behind her. She looked over at the man who,
tall and straight, was standing in the large room watching
her approach. Crazily, then, as her glance rested fleet-
ingly on his handsome mouth, all she could think of was
the way that fabulous mouth had touched hers.

'Good morning, Mr Massingham,' she pulled herself
sharply together to greet him, if her smile had faded
then hoping at least to keep pleasant and civil.

She halted halfway across the carpet, and was aware
of his sharp glance going over her bespectacled face and
shapeless suit. Then, just as she was thinking she had
better sound battle stations because he didn't look best
pleased by what he saw, he suggested affably, 'Come on
in, take a seat,' and indicated a chair at the other side of
his desk.

Leith, still feeling a shade shaky, she had to admit,
was glad to sit down. But she was not a business
executive for nothing, and, since it went without saying
that the time he could spare her from his day was
limited, she placed the buff folder down upon the desk
and without more ado began, 'The Palmer & Pearson
file. There are several firms I intend to approach once

I've got the figures from. . .' She looked up, then her mind went blank. Naylor Massingham, she saw, had his eyes not on the file under discussion, but on her. As she lost the thread entirely, all thought of telling him the work she had done so far went out of her head.

Then he moved, but, instead of moving to take his seat behind his desk as she had expected, he moved to where she was sitting and did not stop until he was level with her.

She was still striving to get herself back together when, to her astonishment, ignoring the file she had placed on his desk, 'Vanity being what it is,' he commented, 'I thought contact lenses were all the go now?'

'I—er. . .' Self-consciously, not to say defensively, Leith touched a hand to her horn-rimmed spectacles. Then, realising that it didn't take much for this man to get to her, she made sterner efforts to get herself more of one piece and, returning her hand to her lap, she drew out of nowhere, 'Not everybody can wear contact lenses,' and added for a touch of authenticity, 'I can't myself.'

She had been astonished before, but the words were barely out of her mouth when, causing her to be absolutely amazed, and with an effrontery she just could not credit, Naylor Massingham did no more than whip her spectacles from off her nose. Instinctively, she shot out a hand to retrieve them, but he was tall, and he was standing, and, while she was an inch or two above average height herself, she was sitting.

She might well have stood too, but he was close by and she had a quick memory of when she had been close up against his body before. Quickly she banished the memory, but as she was about to declare she thought he had a sauce, he had opened the folder that lay on the desk and, taking out a sheet of paper, inspected it through the lenses. In a moment the paper was back in its folder, and he had taken a step away from her.

'You may or may not be able to wear contact lenses, Miss Everett,' he addressed her coolly, 'but you most certainly do not *need* to. These,' he stated positively, 'are plain glass.' Leith was still gasping at his audacity as well as at his discernment when, flicking a glance at the way her chestnut hair was fastened in a repressive knot, he inserted with another glance at her severe hairstyle, 'Now why would a beautiful woman, with equally beautiful hair, try to hide her beauty behind glasses which she clearly doesn't need, try to minimise the beauty of her splendid hair, and also try to detract attention from what I clearly recall is a figure of delightful shape and proportions?'

This man was one on his own! That he'd noticed she'd got a decent figure was to be expected, she supposed, seeing that the lace cotton blouse and culottes she had worn that time she'd gone out to dinner with Travis had touched her contours comfortably. Again she remembered how Naylor Massingham had once held her 'figure of delightful shape and proportions' close up against his body, but again she quickly banished the memory, and decided that that area was far too personal anyhow.

'I need my glasses,' she opted to defend what, if anything at all, was the more impersonal of his charges.

'What for?' he challenged, as she realised she might have guessed he would. 'As sure as hell not to see through, that's a fact!' he ripped into her flatly, and, before she could draw breath, he prodded at the folder that lay on his desk and rapped, 'You read perfectly well from this file—without your glasses—the night I delivered it to your apartment!'

Damn you, she wanted to say, suddenly hating him as she hated realising that while he had watched her reading from the Palmer & Pearson file that night—she had been oblivious that she hadn't been wearing her spectacles—but not so him! 'I sometimes. . .' she began, ready to lie her head off—only to get abruptly cut off before she could perjure herself completely.

'Your mouth gives away the fact that you're not the frigid woman you're making out to be—aside from all the other proof I have!' he needled her by saying curtly.

'What other proof?' she erupted, with more aggressiveness, she realised too late, than sense.

'Apart from your flashing eyes and passionate temper,' he didn't hesitate to remind her, 'you came over anything but frigid when you snuggled up to me the other evening!'

'Sn-snuggled. . .?' she spluttered, but, when she thought about it—and with the memory so recent, it took less than a second—she had to concede that perhaps 'snuggled' wasn't so very far off the mark. In which case she was left with no option but to tell him, a trace arrogantly, it was true, 'I don't wish to discuss it!'

And if she thought she'd get away with that, then she had another think coming, she realised swiftly when, his arrogance topping hers, he rapped bluntly, 'Tough! I'm boss here! While I'm paying for your time, we'll discuss whatever I think necessary,' and if that wasn't enough to send her temper soaring, 'So, for a start, you can begin by telling me why, when I know as fact that two men at least hang their hat up in your home, you're so intent— the glasses, the schoolmarm hairstyle—on living up to the Miss Frostbite label they've pinned on you here?'

'If you must know,' Leith exploded, her anger turning to fury at the way he, with his 'two men at least' comment, had made it sound as though she were some tart, 'I had a bad experience in the last place I worked.'

'Ardis & Co?' he enquired, without question, she realised, having done his homework. Then, as she might have known he would, 'Bad experience—how?' he pressed.

'Someone there—assaulted me, made a grab for me.'

'Sexually, you mean?' he demanded, his expression grave.

'That's what I mean,' she replied, and, since a lot of his aggressiveness seemed to have faded, she felt able to confess, 'It—er—shook me up a bit.'

'Made you afraid of men?' he queried, and looked puzzled as to how that could be when he knew that, since leaving Ardis, she had been to bed with his cousin.

'Not afraid,' she answered honestly, 'just—well, wary, I suppose.'

'I see,' he commented quietly, and, from what Leith could gather, he didn't at all like what he saw. 'So,' he resumed, after a moment, 'you gave notice at Ardis and decided to hide your femin——'

'I didn't give notice,' Leith butted in, having got started on the honesty trail.

'You were dismissed?' he questioned, but by then she had belatedly realised that she had said more than enough. 'Which indicates,' Naylor Massingham went on, waiting no longer for her to answer, 'that the person who assaulted you must be someone quite high up.'

His powers of deduction, Leith felt, were really quite startling. But there was something else which she felt was even more startling. 'You believe me?' she asked in some astonishment. 'I didn't think. . .'

'All the evidence is there, isn't it?' he remarked, and enlightened her as to how he had reached his conclusions. 'Personnel applied to Ardis for a reference—which they freely gave without mentioning anywhere that they had terminated your employment with them. It therefore follows that, since there's nothing in any way the matter with your work, somebody at Ardis is embarrassed by what happened to you—and wants to keep it quiet.' Leith only just managed to stop her jaw from dropping at the astuteness of the man when he continued, 'Having left Ardis and applied for a job here, you then made a conscious decision to dress down your looks and conceal your figure, though not because of any sexual hang-up? Is that right?' he wanted to know when she did not answer.

In actual fact Rosemary had given her the idea about deglamorising herself, but it was with truth, when, feeling forced to reply, Leith answered, 'I've worked hard for my qualifications. I want to be taken seriously, which makes it galling that when I've got a brain, certain types of men try to treat me like some empty-headed bimbo who. . .' She broke off. 'It was you, wasn't it, who saw to it that Paul Fisher got a rocket last Friday?'

Naylor Massingham's mouth tilted fractionally upwards at the corners. 'You *do* have a brain,' he commented.

'Regardless of the Norwood & Chambers contract, I'm good at my job!' Leith retorted.

Unhurriedly he studied her sparking green eyes. 'No one could possibly call you Miss Frostbite if they saw you now,' he drawled and, moving round to sit at his desk, he handed her back her spectacles. Then, before she could put them back on, and to send her thoughts scattering, he directed, 'Don't wear those while I'm around; they offend my sense of beauty.' Leith was still gasping at that when he added, 'To get to the reason why I sent for you——'

'The—er—Palmer & Pearson job,' she interrupted, only then realising that they had barely touched on work the whole time she'd been with him.

He ignored her interruption. 'I've been giving some thought to our—problem,' he stated.

Leith glanced at the folder on the desk. 'Palmer & Pearson?' she queried, and discounted that at once because until things started moving on that contract there were no problems. 'Oh, you mean Norwood &

Chambers,' was the next best she could come up with. 'What——?'

'Are you being *deliberately* obtuse?' Naylor Massingham grated toughly, and, when she stared at him uncomprehendingly, 'I'm talking about the problem of my cousin!' he rapped, and, his tone suddenly far more aggressive, he barked, 'Has he been in touch?'

Brace yourself, Leith, she thought, but could do no other than admit, 'He—phoned from Italy.'

'More than once, I shouldn't wonder,' he grunted, and did not look at all thrilled when she failed to reply. His harsh expression, though, she could cope with. What she didn't like, and what very seriously worried her, was the way, after long moments of giving her a cold-eyed stare, Naylor Massingham should suddenly look at her with such a degree of pleasantness that she just *knew* she wasn't going to like what was going through his brain. There was no fear of his not knowing she did not like it either as, leaning back in his chair, he began easily, 'I propose, after much thought,' he added silkily, charm there in abundance, 'to. . .' he paused, and even smiled '. . .to take you over as *my* girlfriend.'

Instantly Leith was on her feet. 'That lucky you'll never be!' she declared as alarm, a dreadful feeling of alarm, seized her.

She was still trying to cope with what she was beginning to realise was her over-reaction, though she couldn't have said quite why she should feel so alarmed, when he told her coolly, 'You misunderstand me, Miss Everett,' and was on his feet too as, looking arrogantly down at her, he stated bluntly, 'Should I ever be so lucky as you suggest, then, be sure of it, I'd throw away my rabbit's foot,' and having forthrightly left her under no illusion but that should he ever get saddled with her then he would consider his luck had run out, he went on toughly, 'I already know the answer, but, for the record, I want to hear it from you—are you just playing around with Travis for the pure hell of it—or,' his voice had taken on a grim edge, 'are you in love with him?'

'I. . .' Leith began, but, when she was about to declare that she did not love Travis, she suddenly remembered that, in covering for him and Rosemary, she could not be selective.

'Are you?' Naylor Massingham demanded, growing more furious, she realised, the longer she kept him waiting for an answer.

'I'm—fond of Travis—very fond,' she stated, then caught the dangerous glint in her employer's eye that assured her that her prevarication wasn't going down too well. When she saw his hands at his sides clench into aggressive fists, 'No,' she found she had answered truthfully.

'You're not in love with him and you have no intention of marrying him?' he insisted.

'He hasn't asked me. . .' she tried prevarication again, but broke off when, his jaw jutting at a tough angle, Naylor took a menacing step towards her. 'No,' she replied.

'Which must mean that, regardless of the fact that he's so wound up over you he can't think straight, you're only playing around with him for the pure hell of it.'

Strangely then, at the thought of the heartless female he made her sound, Leith felt an almost overwhelming compulsion to tell him the truth. But she couldn't, and a moment later she was asking herself what on earth had got into her that whatever he thought of her should bother her!

'Well?' he rapped.

She shrugged. 'If you like,' she replied, and knew she had infuriated him when he thrust his hands into his pockets as if to prevent himself from taking hold of her and shaking the daylights out of her.

'Women like you turn my stomach!' he grated harshly, and, clearly fed up to the teeth with her, 'I don't know why I don't just terminate your employment and get rid of you!'

And *that* made Leith instantly furious. No man would get dismissed for that same reason—she'd bet on it! 'Because you're afraid that, jobless, I might set up home with Travis!' she exploded spiritedly. It was immaterial then in her fury that there was never any such possibility.

Fury, she was swiftly made to realise, was not limited solely to her when he demanded savagely, 'What the *hell* do you mean by that?'

Leith was angry enough not to back down. 'You wouldn't want me for a cousin-in-law, by the sound of it.'

'Too bloody true!' he snarled, but cooled down marginally, though that dangerous glint was still around somewhere when he added, 'But since you've just said you've no intention of marrying my cousin—this is what you're going to do.' Briefly he paused, then, 'The next time you see him, while letting him down gently, you will make sure that he knows you don't love him.'

'You think I'm capable of it—letting him down gently?' Leith queried, sarcasm getting the better of her.

Much good did it do! Ignoring her comment as if she hadn't spoken, Naylor Massingham continued, 'From there you will tell Travis that, having met me, you can't help but be interested in me.'

'He's supposed to believe this fairy story?' Leith butted in.

She was again ignored. Though this time when he went on, he was to leave her speechless and open-mouthed. 'That done,' he went on determinedly, 'and for as long as it takes for him to get you out of his system, you will be my girlfriend. And,' he insisted threateningly, when it seemed she might find her voice to make some vigorous protest, 'if you value your job, which I'm sure you do, you won't breathe a word to him that it's all a put-up affair.'

Leith began to recover from feeling shaken to realise that things had gone too far now for her to confess everything, but in any case she couldn't do that, not when Rosemary and Travis were so insistent on secrecy. What else was plain, though, was that she had wasted her time in trying to turn the tables on Naylor Massingham by hinting that, jobless, she might set up home with Travis. Naylor was calling her bluff, and there was not a thing she could do about it—the swine!

'There—must be some other way,' she voiced her thoughts out loud, and, as the thought occurred, 'I can tell Travis that I don't want to see him again without going in for this—this charade.' Naylor was shaking his head before she had finished.

'I told you to end your relationship with him before, but you didn't.' Leith opened her mouth to interrupt, but he went straight on without pause. 'Which has given me time to realise that the way I've outlined is the way it has to be. I now see that Travis is so smitten that he wouldn't accept anything but that, meeting me for the first time when I called at your apartment, you at once became very much attracted to me. You thereafter saw me daily here, and. . .'

'It's all one-sided, is it?' Leith cut in shrewishly. 'This—*attraction*?'

Again he shook his head. 'That's the whole point— regardless, Miss Everett, that both you and I know that you're never going to marry him anyway, Travis, who cares deeply for his family,' as you do, Leith could well have inserted, 'is only going to take it on the chin and let you go, by learning that the person you *do* love is a member of his family, who loves you in return.'

'You, in fact!'

'Precisely.'

Leith did not like it one tiny bit. She was aware that Naylor Massingham was watching her. She knew he was waiting for her to agree, and it was desperation, pure and simple, she thought, that made her remember the elegant blonde he had been dining with that particular night. 'What about your *other* girlfriend?' she challenged hostilely, oddly feeling the most peculiar reluctance to state the blonde's name.

'Girlfriend?' he queried.

It was clear to Leith then that Olinda Bray was one of many. 'Olinda Bray.' She decided she wasn't reluctant to remind him of Olinda's name in any way, shape or form. 'Olinda,' she brought out her name again for good measure, 'seemed to find you attractive the other night.'

'You know how it is,' Naylor shrugged.

'Either you've got it or you haven't?'

To her surprise, he actually grinned—a most shattering grin. Why she should suddenly feel like bursting out laughing, Leith had no idea. She firmly suppressed any such notion, however. This wasn't funny. She was being blackmailed and, because of her promise to Travis never to breathe a word about the woman he truly did love, she could not do a thing about it.

'It seems,' she told him stonily, 'that I haven't any option but to do as you say.' She flicked a glance at him. His grin had gone, and he was returning her hating look with no quarter given. That annoyed her—in fact his whole attitude annoyed her. 'One thing more——' She thought she might as well get in while she was at it.

'Well?' he barked, clearly not ecstatic that she thought she could lay down conditions.

Leith was past caring. 'I'm not in line to go to bed with you in order to keep my job!' she told him bluntly.

She read her answer before he so much as opened his mouth. It was all there in the lofty, superior look he threw her. He had no need, no need at all to say that, beautiful though he might have mentioned he thought her, she just did not hold those sort of charms for him— which was what he more or less did say when he drawled, 'Would you think me dreadfully ungallant should I mop my brow and tell you—that's a relief?'

Swine, in her book, was much, much too good for him! And had Leith any compunction about what she was doing on her own behalf, because it was for sure that, having given her an ultimatum, Naylor Massingham would create hell on the day he learned— as, sure as her name was not Rosemary, one day he must—that he had claimed her as his girlfriend for nothing, then that compunction vanished without trace. There was only one assurance she wanted.

'Do I have your promise that, regardless of what happens, regardless of—er—whether you like it or not, at the end of this—farce, I'll still have my job?'

He looked at her levelly. 'You have my word,' he told her. That was all she waited to hear. The Palmer & Pearson file she had brought up with her was forgotten as she swung round and headed for the door. 'One more thing!' his voice stopped her before she made it through to the other side.

Leith halted and turned round. 'Yes?' she queried coldly.

'It's obvious to me, since you can't possibly be paying all the mortgage on your flat without help, that my cousin must be paying something towards it.' Her fury was still on an upward spiral as he announced, 'From now on, that charge will be mine.'

Had he been standing within striking distance, then, as her fury overflowed, Leith was fairly certain she would have hit him. As it was, it was left to her to verbally let him know what she thought of his offer to help her out with her mortgage.

'Like hell it will!' she exploded, and, ramming her glasses on to her nose, she slammed furiously out of his office. When, she thought, had there ever been a moment when she had been unsure that she disliked him? Dislike him? She positively hated the swine!

CHAPTER FIVE

WHEN Thursday of that week came round, Leith was beginning to think she had never worked so hard. She had worked hard last week, but there seemed to her to be more work than ever landing on her desk this week. Perhaps it was just as well Rosemary was still not back. The hours she was working, she was left with little time for popping across the corridor for coffee and a chat, let alone for socialising.

Should she get the chance to socialise, she thought, a second later. She was still quietly simmering from her interview with Naylor Massingham last Monday. He of the, 'I propose, after much thought, to take you over as *my* girlfriend'! So, if she was supposed to be his girlfriend, what was she doing staying home nights? Not that she wanted him to contact her—perish the thought! In any case, she was too busy attacking the contents of her briefcase when she got home to have gone out with him, even if he *had* asked her—which he hadn't.

Knowing him, though, he wouldn't ask, would he? Tell, order, command, but never ask. 'From now on, that charge will be mine,' he'd had the utter nerve to *tell* her. As if she'd allow any man to pay her mortgage!

When Leith took time off from being absolutely furious with Naylor Massingham and his high-handed behaviour, though, she experienced odd moments of wanting to tell him openly that she was not, and never had been, romantically interested in his cousin. Those moments did not last for long, however, because she was soon hearing again his silky, and infuriating, declaration that he was taking her over as *his* girlfriend.

It crossed her mind that perhaps she should, despite her employer's '. . .if you value your job, you won't breathe a word to him that it's all a put-up affair', explain some of it to Travis. Not that she'd seen or heard from him again since his phone call from Italy on Sunday. Somehow, though, and it was a complete mystery to her why, she felt an odd sort of reluctance to do anything of the kind. Could it be some odd kind of loyalty to Naylor Massingham? Was it fear of losing her job? She definitely couldn't afford to lose her job, that much *was* certain.

She decided to give up thinking about it—she was getting her own back on Mr Lord-Almighty anyway, wasn't she? There was no need whatsoever for him to 'take her over'—she knew that, and Travis knew that, and Naylor Massingham would create merry hell when *he* eventually knew that. But he'd got it coming, and she—she'd got his word that, when it was all over, she'd still have her job.

'Are you working late again tonight, Leith?' Her assistant, standing at her elbow with a query, brought her away from such thoughts; and sent her thoughts off down another avenue.

'Tonight, Jimmy,' she replied, 'I'm leaving at five.'

She dealt with his query and recalled how, when she had been going over everything Naylor had said, including his certainty that someone else must be chipping in to pay her mortgage, she had got round to accepting that she just could not afford to go on living where she was. It was useless to start calling her irresponsible brother a few names—he'd always been the same, and she'd known that, love him though she did, when they had moved to London. Her mistake had been to think that being a part-owner of a property might change him.

Needing to think very deeply about her situation,

however, Leith pushed thoughts of Sebastian from her and got down to serious thought.

Nothing very brilliant had come to her, though, until, not thinking of her problem in so much depth, she was doing some washing-up when she thought of Rosemary and, suddenly, of how Rosemary was renting *her* flat. In minutes, Leith knew what she had to do. Another ten minutes later she had it all worked out. Rosemary had once told her the amount she was paying in rent. If she could get the same amount for her flat, then that would cover the mortgage. It would mean moving to a less salubrious area, of course, but the answer clearly lay in her renting accommodation which was much cheaper.

She had spent her lunch-hours of the two previous days in talking to letting agents. At five o'clock that Thursday evening she left her office, noticed sourly that her 'boyfriend's' Jaguar was in the car park, and drove off to view a flat that was within her means.

'It's very nice,' she complimented the pleasant person who, although not vacating immediately, was taking a teaching job up north later in the year and wanted everything organised well before then.

'It's quite large for around here,' the woman told her, and, even though it was nowhere near as large as Leith's present flat, nor in the area that she was used to either, she was in a 'beggars can't be choosers' situation. The rent was right, if nothing else was.

'I'd like to take it,' she made up her mind on the spot, not wanting to return to her larger flat and start to have doubts.

Over a cup of tea, the outgoing lessee imparted all the rules of the sub-let. And, as she had invited her to have another look around, it was almost seven o'clock by the time Leith turned into the select avenue of her present home.

Her thoughts were on the fact that it would be three

months before she could move into her new abode, as she drove up the avenue. That meant that as well as the cheque she had just written for her first month's rent on her new accommodation, she would have to find three months' mortgage from somewhere. She decided to look on the positive side. Three months would give her a chance to pack up both her belongings and her brother's—and perhaps whoever she found to take on her flat would pay a month's rent in advance too.

Of course they would, she thought bracingly, and, feeling more cheerful suddenly, she turned into the driveway of her apartment block—and saw a Jaguar parked where no Jaguar was normally parked! There was a man seated behind the steering-wheel. Their glances met—and locked.

Crikey! Leith saw at once that he was furious about something! She drove past and round to the garages at the rear. She would look forward to changing her address, she decided. The only problem there, though, since she would have to let Personnel at Vasey's know where she had moved to, was that her employer would have no trouble in finding her at her new address either!

She garaged her car and thought briefly of entering the apartment block by the rear entrance. Was she such a coward? She'd seen Naylor furious before, hadn't she? She secured her garage door and, having decided to walk round to the front of the building to find out what Naylor was so furious about, she turned around—and found she had no need to go anywhere. Naylor, tall, dark, and not looking any sweeter, was right there towering over her.

She opened her mouth—he got in first. 'Where the blazes have you been?' he demanded before she could blink.

The nerve! The very nerve of him! 'That's none of your business!' she let fly.

'Like hell it isn't!' he exploded. 'Travis had enough work to last three weeks but, on account of you, he must have worked like the devil. He's back in town!'

Knowing full well that it wasn't on her account that Travis had worked so hard, Leith shrugged. 'He probably called while I was out,' she replied carelessly—and had her ears blasted for her trouble.

'He hasn't! Dammit, I've been parked watching the entrance since six!'

The idea of the lofty Naylor Massingham sitting impatiently outside her apartment block for an hour was one which Leith found quite pleasing—so much so that she almost broke into a smile. Resolutely she held the smile down and, since he was being so aggressive, her own tone was short as she snapped nastily, 'What are *you* doing here anyway?'

'Don't be shy—call me Naylor!' he thundered, and suddenly Leith's sense of humour got the better of her, and she burst out laughing. He seemed arrested by her laughter, she saw, as she watched his glance go from the merriment in her eyes to her laughing mouth. And then, even while she was making valiant efforts to control herself, because for certain he was going to set about strangling her at any moment, after some seconds of looking at her as if staggered, suddenly, and to her amazement, he was seeing the funny side of it also—and he was laughing too!

How laughter changed him, she thought. But when her heart actually did a little flutter to see that mouth, which she had always liked—despite its owner—turning up in laughter, she half turned from him and started to walk towards the rear entrance of the building.

She was not totally surprised when he fell into step with her. 'Come in—in case you weren't going to,' she invited.

'Too kind!' he murmured, and was there beside her

every step of the way until they reached the door of her flat.

She had guessed by that time that, since he hadn't yet stated why he'd waited an hour to see her, he was saving what he'd come to tell her until they were inside her flat. Perhaps he'd come to tell her he'd changed his mind about his decision that she was to be his 'girlfriend' until Travis was over her, she mused, and, since courtesy cost nothing, she invited him in.

She was more than a little astounded, however, that, as Naylor stood facing her in the hall of her home, she should suddenly feel breathless and find that she was extending that courtesy even further. 'I'm starving,' she heard her own voice volunteer and, incredibly, 'I don't suppose you've eaten yet either?'

If he was as surprised as she at what amounted to an invitation to share her meal, then he did not show it, but said merely, 'Want me to lay the table?'

Half an hour later he was seated on her couch reading a financial magazine she subscribed to while in the kitchen a cheesecake was defrosting in the microwave, and a home-made lasagne warming up in the oven. Leith, having popped along to her bedroom to take her hair out of the knot she had worn it in all day, was having serious thoughts about her actions—inviting him for a meal, for goodness' sake! Anybody would think she was pleased to see him!

Aware, as she most certainly was, that she could not be pleased to see him—grief, if past experience was anything to go by, they'd no doubt be going for each other's throats before the meal was half over—Leith returned to the kitchen and prepared some salad.

She was in the middle of making a salad dressing when someone rang her doorbell. For a sweet moment she thought it might be Sebastian come home—but Sebastian had his key. She knew that Rosemary wasn't back yet either, and, with Naylor not long ago saying that Travis was back, Leith realised that logically there was every chance that her caller could be her guest's cousin.

Oh, crumbs! she thought as, quickly rinsing a smear of olive oil from her hands, she heard the bell ring again. What was she supposed to do—how was she supposed to act? Naylor thought Travis was her lover, and she couldn't tell Naylor that he wasn't—not without bringing in Rosemary across the corridor. Yet Travis—if it was him—had exacted a promise from her that she mustn't breathe a word about Rosemary.

Swiftly before whoever it was could ring again, Leith sped from the kitchen. But she discovered she had delayed too long, for as she reached the hall, there before her, and as cool as you like, was Naylor. And, just as if he too suspected her caller was Travis, he had taken the diabolical liberty of answering her door himself.

But with her view of her caller blocked by the open door and her guest, Leith was in too much of a dilemma just then to be too infuriated by the liberty he had taken. Then she recognised Travis's voice as, plainly startled, he questioned, 'Good heavens! What are you doing here?' Clearly Travis, unlike his cousin, would never think of noticing familiar-looking vehicles in the parking area!

Had she been expecting Naylor to be stuck for words or, now that the moment of carrying out the plan he had put to her had arrived, ducking it, then she was disappointed on both counts. For, proving that he cared for his family every bit as much as it had seemed, he said, 'Hello, Travis, come in. Leith's in the kitchen cooking my dinner.'

That, she thought, was as good an idea as any, and on silent feet she went as swiftly as she had come back to her kitchen. It was not a complete surprise when a minute later Travis, with Naylor leading the way, walked into her kitchen.

'Travis!' she smiled. He looks tired—and worried—she thought, and, regardless of Naylor watching, she could do no other than go over to Travis and kiss his cheek. 'How nice to see you.' She carried on smiling, ignoring Naylor's menacing expression. And when Travis seemed absolutely stumped for words, she could do no other than fill what would have been an awkward silence with, 'I could probably make the lasagne go three ways if. . .'

At last Travis started to recover from his surprise, and, Leith realised, his doomed hopes. 'No, thanks, Leith. I had something to eat not long ago. I—er—just thought I'd look in to tell you I was back.' Oh, the dear love, thought Leith, having just realised that, heartsick for a sight of Rosemary, he must have been hoping that Rosemary was back and that she might, if asked, come over for a cup of coffee.

'Did you have a——?' good trip, Leith might have said, but as if thinking he'd given them enough time to sort themselves out, Naylor was butting in, and positively flabbergasting her by what he chose to interrupt with!

'I do hope that's not my lasagne I can smell burning, my dear,' and while she moved swiftly to check the oven and to find that not a thing was burning, Naylor was saying, 'We'll see you at the weekend, Travis.' *We!* 'Actually, you arrived just as I was about to invite Leith to Parkwood. You'd like that, wouldn't you, Leith?' he had the unmitigated nerve to put her on the spot.

'The lasagne's fine,' she murmured as she played for time and thought of the three months' mortgage she had to find and how impossible she would find it to pay one months' mortgage, let alone three, if she didn't have a job. Which she wouldn't, she realised, if she didn't buck her ideas up and play this according to Mr Naylor I-hold-all-the-aces Massingham. 'It sounds very nice.' She smiled, and didn't care a bit then that when it came to leading Travis up the garden path, she was doing a little garden path trail-blazing herself. Thank goodness she'd thought to get Naylor's word about her job.

'I'll leave you to your lasagne,' Travis was saying as she tuned back in.

'I'll see you at the weekend, then,' Leith said lightly, and was once more wanting to do something of a pugilistic nature to her employer when, just as though he lived there, he went to the door with Travis and saw him out.

Naylor was soon back. 'For a man who's got it so badly, Travis took that very well,' he began admiringly. 'I thought he'd be man enough to——' but Leith had other things on her mind and wasted no time cutting in and going into orbit.

'How *dare* you invite me to Parkwood in front of him? How——?'

'You'd rather I'd done it behind his back?' Naylor replied to her salvo with an aggressive one of his own.

'You gave me no chance to refuse!' Leith erupted. 'No chance whatsoever. You——'

'It never occurred to me, given I'd already got your agreement to be my woman, that you could possibly have any objection!' he tossed back toughly, and, if she wanted more, 'You can say "no" whenever you like!' he hurled at her aggressively.

Yes, and lose my job, she fumed belligerently. Swine! she thought with impotent rage, and took exception on another front. 'What are Travis's parents going to say?' she questioned hostilely.

'About what?'

Again Leith came close to hitting him. 'Don't you

think they'll think it funny that you're the one taking me to his home, and not Travis?'

'Why should they? Travis has said nothing to his family about any Leith Everett, so they won't have heard your name before. For that matter, he's never said anything to me about you either. I only found out about you when I saw his car parked outside that night.' A muscle suddenly jerked in his jaw, and his tone was all at once arctic. 'He's never ever mentioned that night to me since, so as far as he's aware,' he rapped cuttingly, 'I could think you were nothing more than an easy one-nighter for him!'

Her breath caught. *Blunt* wasn't in it! 'Thanks!' she hissed through clenched teeth, and would see him in hell before she fed him. Then she discovered he'd gone off any idea of tucking into the delights of her home-made lasagne anyway as, without another word, he turned and headed out of the kitchen.

Unable to wait to slam the door hard shut behind him, she followed him into the hall. He had the door open and his back to her when, her brother's hat obviously catching his eye, he halted, stretched out a hand to it, then turned to where Leith, antagonistically-expressioned, stood, obviously wanting him out of her flat.

Suddenly the deerstalker came whizzing through the air, and as, instinctively, she caught it, he bellowed, 'And get rid of that!'

Sebastian's hat was back on the coat fixture when Leith left for her office the next morning. She was still furious with Naylor. How could he, even if he did have what he thought was some pretty overwhelming evidence, think she might be anybody's easy one-nighter? It—hurt.

She mutinied on and off against him all that morning, and for most of the afternoon. Arrogant swine, she fumed, and hoped with all she had that he'd gone to bed hungry last night. He wouldn't, though—not him.

When Leith was not mutinying against him, she was alternately engaged—while still producing a fair output of work—in wondering if he had really been serious about taking her to Parkwood to meet Travis's parents this weekend.

It had just gone four that afternoon when she had her answer. The phone in her office rang, and Jimmy answered. 'It's for you!' he said smartly, and handed the phone over to her with such promptness that she knew whoever was on the other end was someone important.

Expecting it to be someone high up in one of the many companies she had dealings with—though it was unusual for Jimmy not to supply her with a name—she announced efficiently, 'Leith Everett.'

'Be ready at eleven tomorrow morning!' rapped a voice she would know anywhere, his tone not one whit pleasanter than it had been when he'd left her flat last night.

'Yes, sir!' she retorted snappily, and banged the phone down hard. A second later she was remembering that she, who had once vowed never to call Naylor Massingham 'sir', had just done so.

Damn him, damn him to hell! she was thinking aggressively, when all at once she caught Jimmy's eyes on her. She could tell at once that he knew who her caller had been and, from his expression, that his intelligence was working overtime as to why the head of the Massingham empire should ring her personally. If Jimmy added that fact to the fact that Mr Massingham had wanted to see her last Monday, then heaven knew what his fertile mind would come up with!

Jimmy, a world of conjecture in his face, opened his mouth, and Leith thought it time to put a stop to his speculations before he went any further. 'Don't ask!' she warned him severely.

He closed his mouth. Then suddenly a wide grin split his face. 'Wouldn't dream of it, honest, Leith,' he replied.

Leith was busily sorting through her wardrobe, finding unexpectedly that, while she had always had an ability to make decisions, she was dithering over what to take with her to Parkwood tomorrow. She was still not at all happy about going, and frequently wondered what in fact she was doing packing anyway. Inevitably it came down to the same couple of answers—her mortgage, her job.

Heavens! she thought, and was suddenly so impatient with herself that, seeing it was only for one night, for goodness' sake, she grabbed hold of a favourite dress and folded that into her case along with some trousers and a spare lightweight sweater. Then her phone rang.

'It's Travis—are you on your own?' he wanted to know.

For a moment Leith wondered who the dickens he thought she had with her, then she remembered Naylor had been with her last night when Travis had called. Perhaps he thought she and Naylor were so enamoured of each other that he was always there. 'I'm on my own,' she answered, and was thinking on her feet when Travis followed on with something that was only natural.

'I was shaken rigid when Naylor opened your door to me last night.'

'I've—er—seen quite a bit of him since I met him when he called for you that time,' Leith managed, the ever-present 'if you value your job' threat there in her head again.

'I gathered that much, you both working in the same building and everything.' Travis, to her amazement, swallowed without hesitation that she and Naylor saw each other frequently at work—and were drawn to each other! Then, to give her basically honest soul more to contend with, he went on, 'Naylor must be fairly serious about you, Leith,' and asked, 'How do you feel about him?'

'It's—er—early days yet.' She avoided telling him what an out-and-out swine she thought his cousin was, adding quickly, 'What makes you think he's serious?'

'He's never brought any woman home before,' Travis replied promptly, and to her horror tacked on warmly, 'I couldn't be more pleased that it's you, Leith.'

'Oh, Travis!' she blurted out helplessly.

'I know, I know, it's early days, as you said—but you're just not the type to let him go this far if you had any serious doubts.' And, while she was wondering how in creation she should answer that, Travis, his own problems clearly paramount, was going on. 'I know this is a difficult time for you, and I know that you'd hate like hell to lie to Naylor—though I sincerely hope you won't have to—but I can still rely on you to keep quiet about Rosemary and me, can't I?' Leith hesitated, and was sorely tempted then to tell Travis the whole of it. Oddly, though, even when she opened her mouth to betray her pact with Naylor, she found that she could not betray him. 'I *can* rely on you, Leith?' Travis was insisting.

'Of course. You know that,' she replied, and discovered that Travis, more interested in his love-life than hers, wanted to talk about Rosemary and how much he missed seeing her and the fact that he had been so lonesome for her that he'd phoned her flat several times yesterday evening and, receiving no reply, had realised she must still be at her parents' home.

'I didn't dare ring her direct,' he went on, 'which is why I turned up at your place. I know you'll think I've got no end of a cheek, but what I was hoping was that you'd ring Rosemary for me and, if her parents weren't about, pass the phone over to me.'

Oh, poor Travis, Leith thought, her sympathies going out to him for the terrible time he was having. 'I don't think you have a cheek at all,' she told him gently.

'If you're sure. . .' he began, then asked, 'You wouldn't ring Rosemary for me now, would you? Just to tell her I'm thinking of her.'

She rang Rosemary shortly after Travis had rung off, and conveyed his message to her. 'That's nice,' Rosemary replied carefully, and Leith understood then that she couldn't talk freely.

Leith felt more than a bit dissatisfied with life when she went to bed that night. She was fond of Rosemary, and appreciated her sensitivity where her parents were concerned, and she also appreciated her inner turmoil when her own beliefs were being put to the test. But Travis had been marvellously patient for months and months now—couldn't she find a way to put him out of the private hell he was in?

She felt she was in a private hell of her own on Saturday morning while she waited for Naylor to call. Again she was questioning why in creation she was giving in to his edicts, but, when she received nothing new in the way of an answer, rebellion set in.

That rebellion caused her to be half inclined to scrape her hair back in a 'schoolmarm' hairstyle, and to be wearing her heavy hornrimmed spectacles when His Lordship called. She decided against it in the end, not because she was afraid of any brutish remarks he might—not might, would, she corrected—make when he saw her, but because, from where she viewed it, this was going to be a tough enough weekend without her inviting hassle before it began.

Naylor did not keep her waiting, but rang her doorbell with a few minutes to go before eleven. 'Good morning,' she greeted him stiffly, letting him into her flat and preceding him into her sitting-room. She had one or two questions she wanted to ask him before they went anywhere.

She took a calming breath and turned, and was put off her stroke for a moment when she saw his glance flicking over her slim and erect carriage, taking in the elegant and attractive navy-trimmed white outfit she wore. He was dressed more casually, and, just as he looked good— and then some—in a business suit, Leith realised that to some women his tall, casually clad self was quite something more.

'I've got an overnight bag packed, but before we go——' she took a hold on herself to begin, then found that he had something he wanted to say too—and that he didn't mind cutting across what she was saying, to say it.

'What did you tell Travis?' he sliced in apropos of nothing.

'When?' she questioned, feeling her palms already starting to itch—and she hadn't been in his company five minutes yet!

'You're saying he hasn't been in touch since he left this flat on Thursday?'

'Do you want a blow-by-blow account?' His aggression fired hers. 'Or will you settle for the fact that he now thinks I find you pretty irresistible?'

Naylor studied her silently and hostilely for some seconds, mutual enmity rife. Then, ever a man to answer selectively only what he cared to, he asked, 'Where's your bag?'

'Just a minute!' She refused to budge until she'd got one or two matters in order, and, ignoring the fact that he looked ready to go and hunt up her bag himself if she didn't soon move herself, 'Is it all right for you to invite me to Mr and Mrs Hepwood's home?' she asked for starters, and braved his acid glance that said he'd hardly be likely to issue an invitation if it wasn't.

'Just in case you don't know—though I'm sure you do,' he threw at her, 'I made my home with my aunt and uncle from the age of ten. Their home is my home,' he went on coldly, 'and they'd be extremely hurt if they thought I believed otherwise.'

Leith could imagine that would be the case, and, even though she knew the answer to a question that just then came to her, for clarification's sake, she asked it just the same. 'But you don't live with them now?'

'It's convenient for me to have a flat in town,' he replied shortly.

I'll bet it is, Leith thought, but couldn't understand at all why she should all at once feel something that felt mightily like jealousy, at the sudden mental picture of a stream of blondes passing through his flat. 'How are you going to introduce me?' she asked tartly, denying most vigorously that she could be jealous in any remote way.

'As my girlfriend—what else?'

'You've no compunction about deceiving them?'

'After all they've done for me,' he bit toughly, 'I'd have far more compunction if I allowed their youngest and much-thought-of son to ruin his life over some female who obviously doesn't care a damn for him!'

'Has anyone ever told you how perfectly detestable you are?' Leith snapped angrily—and realised she could go on in the same vein until she was blue in the face and it still wouldn't dent him.

Though suddenly his toughness had gone and mockery was all about him as, rocking back on his heels, he stared into her furious flashing green eyes and taunted, 'Oh, but you're beautiful when you're angry!'

Parkwood was a large house set in its own grounds and was situated in a rural area of woodlands and fields, and

was, to Leith's mind, quite idyllic. They arrived there
with about twenty minutes to go before lunch, which
was just time for general introductions and for Leith to
be shown her room, wash her hands and rejoin Naylor,
Cicely and Guthrie Hepwood, and Travis downstairs.
And, contrary to her belief, she found she was enjoying
the atmosphere at Parkwood.

'Naylor tells me you're one of the best executives in
your particular line,' Cicely Hepwood, a neat and gentle
woman, remarked at one point during the meal.

Leith shot a glance at Naylor, seated next to her, who
wasn't even a tinge pink around the ears at his aunt's
revealing what, since there were others in her particular
line who were far more senior, must surely be a lie.
'That's probably why he instructs my head of department to keep me so busy,' she answered lightly, and
then, with a jolt of astonishment, wondered if Naylor *did*
have anything to do with the multitude of files that
landed on her desk every day. She looked at him again
and saw this time that he was watching her. 'Do you?'
she asked, meaning, did the instructions come from you?

He had no trouble grasping her meaning, she saw, and
he even smiled as he replied, 'You're too sharp, Leith.
You weren't supposed to know—I have this yen to keep
you out of mischief.'

Devil! she thought, but, because they were in company, she smiled back at him. But she hadn't missed
what *he* meant! His idea, she realised, was that if he saw
to it that she had enough work to keep her occupied
both at work and at home, there would be little time left
over, if she wanted to keep on top of her job, for any
social life with Travis.

'Poor Leith!' Travis entered the conversation. 'Just
because Naylor's a workaholic, he's trying to make you
one too!'

Leith saw Naylor give his cousin a sharp glance. 'No

chance,' she stated swiftly on a light laugh, and quickly
dismissed the subject by turning to her host with a query
about the wine that went so well with the meal. 'Is this
one of the wines you import, Mr Hepwood?' she asked—
and suddenly, as everyone looked a trace amused, any
tension she had imagined to be there magically
disappeared.

'My uncle wouldn't allow a bottle from any other
merchant near his cellar,' Naylor explained good-
humouredly, and on that light note the meal came to an
end.

There followed a few minutes' discussion where it
seemed Cicely Hepwood had been all set to cancel an
arrangement she and her husband had to visit a sick
friend in hospital that afternoon.

'You'll do no such thing,' declared Naylor. 'You'd no
idea I'd be bringing Leith home when you made your
arrangements. Besides, Leith and I were planning to
take a walk.'

It was news to Leith, but she certainly didn't want her
hosts to deprive some unfortunate sick person of their
company. 'That's what we planned,' she agreed, and a
few minutes later Cicely was talking of leaving for the
hospital in half an hour.

'What do you intend to do this afternoon, Travis?' she
asked her younger son, despite her cheerful and pleasant
tone, with a trace of anxiety which Leith recognised
from having seen her own mother trying to be similarly
tactful with Sebastian on occasions.

Leith waited, very much wanting to invite Travis to
join her and Naylor on their walk, but one glance at
Naylor—who seemed determined not to invite Travis
himself—told her that she'd regret it if she did.

'I'll find something to do,' he replied eventually.

'You'll—hmm—be in to dinner?' his mother enquired
lightly.

'You're not fussing are you, old love?' teased Travis.

Cicely laughed lightly. 'I'm going upstairs to change,' she told him.

Leith thought that idea, to change, was quite a good one in view of Naylor's stated intention that they were taking a walk.

'If you'll excuse me,' she murmured, and followed her hostess out of the room.

Upstairs she changed into trousers and a light sweater and some flat-heeled shoes. So far things had gone much better than she had expected. Oh, she hadn't missed Naylor's eyes on her a time or two when she exchanged some comment with Travis—but surely he didn't expect her to ignore him!

Naylor was waiting for her when twenty minutes later she went back down the stairs. She saw his glance go over her, ending at the tips of her sensible shoes, and wondered if she was in for some punishing ten-mile hike. Strange how her heart should give a little flutter. Well, it had been some while since she'd walked ten miles in one go—or even five, for that matter, she excused her fluttering heart.

'Ready?' he enquired, quite pleasantly, she thought, as her heart gave another peculiar flutter.

'Do we need to say cheerio to anyone?' she asked.

'If you're thinking of Travis, forget it!' he snarled grimly.

Her palm itched. Without comment, she marched past him out into the sunlight while she still could. He fell into step with her before she had marched more than ten yards down the drive.

'We'll go round past the stables and cut across the fields,' he told her.

'Delighted!'

The next ten minutes passed in utter silence. At the end of those ten minutes, though, they had taken a turn to the right, then one to the left, and it was apparent that Naylor knew his way around the area.

He had no doubt played here when he was a child, climbed trees, even swam in the river that. . . Abruptly, Leith's thoughts ceased. His parents had died when he was only ten, she recalled, and, as her heart went out to him, all enmity in her against him ended. She doubted then that he had felt very much like climbing trees or swimming in the river for some long while after he had lost his parents.

'Naylor,' she turned to him with his name on her lips, oddly, his pain her pain at that moment.

'She knows my name!' he commented wryly, and at that moment Leith realised that that was the first time she had used it.

'The "sir" slipped out the other day,' she told him.

'I guessed,' he replied, and suddenly gave her a lop-sided grin—and all at once Leith discovered she was feeling most unexpectedly lighthearted.

But that would never do. She sought round for some sobering thought. 'I—er—forgot to ask you about the Palmer & Pearson——' It was as far as she got.

'I never discuss work outside the office,' he cut her off.

Open-mouthed, Leith turned her head to stare at him. He met her incredulous stare blandly, for all the world as if he had no recollection whatsoever of bringing her the Palmer & Pearson file *outside the office*, of discussing the Norwood & Chambers contract *outside the office*, of his threats in relation to her job *outside the office*. For all the world too as though a man who everyone knew— even his cousin who didn't work with him—was a workaholic, had never taken work home, it was most definitely a bit much.

'So,' Leith swallowed down at least four contradictions

she could have lobbed at him, and queried sarcastically instead, 'what *would* you like to talk about?'

She fully expected him to ignore her sarcastic question, or, in his delightfully blunt fashion, tell her he was out for a walk, not an idle chinwag, when, to cause her to falter in her stride, 'How about—where you'd been last Thursday while I waited outside your flat for you to come home?'

Startled again, Leith turned to stare at him. To hear him tell it you'd think they'd had a date and she'd turned up late! 'I. . . B. . .' she began, got herself together from his impudence, and could see no reason not to reveal, 'I went looking for somewhere else to live.'

'What's wrong with where you are now?' He either didn't believe her, or was so unused to accepting answers unquestioningly that it was second nature for him to delve into the nitty-gritty.

Leith's right hand started to itch again. 'There's nothing wrong with where I live,' she halted in her tracks to tell him shortly, 'except, as you at once realised,' she inserted loftily, 'that the mortgage is beyond my means. I went looking for somewhere cheaper to——'

'I've told you I'll attend to that!' he cut her off sharply—and infuriatingly.

'I heard you!' she retorted, her pride up in arms.

'Huh!' he grunted, and, she swiftly realised, must have done a lightning analysis of what she had said, because in his next breath he was commenting aggressively, 'So you've definitely decided to throw Travis over?'

You're going too fast for me, thought Leith, but her voice was every bit as aggressive as his as she spat, 'I'm not with you!'

'Oh, come on!' he rapped, his chin jutting, aggression too mild a term for it. 'Or,' he demanded harshly, 'do you have someone other than me lined up to pay your mortgage?'

'Why, you. . .!' Leith yelled, and as fury which she just could not contain spiralled out of control, her right hand arced through the air, and even as she hit him with all her strength, she was still yelling, 'Since it seems to be taking so long to sink in, you can bank on it—whoever pays my mortgage, you're far, far at the back of the queue!' With that, careless of his obvious amazement that someone of her slender weight could not only pack such a punch but dare to do so, she spun rapidly round and raced back the way she had come.

She guessed he was probably still staring after her, but she didn't care then about anything but the fact that he should have such a low opinion of her. How dared he think what he did? How dared he believe that she'd been taking money from Travis to pay her way? How dared he think it, let alone say it, that she had other men to settle her bills?

She was still going full pelt when Parkwood came into view. How dared he talk to her as though she was some tramp? How dared he?

On the rear lawn not too far from the house stood a summerhouse. Leith skirted round it, saw as she neared the house that the french doors of the drawing-room were open, but was in too much of an emotional uproar to realise that she could take a short cut.

She went in by the front door and upstairs to her room; and was still being torn apart by her emotions. How dared he? she mourned as she sank down on her bed and gasped for breath, and knew then that Naylor Massingham's low opinion of her wouldn't hurt anywhere near as much as it did, had she not just realised that she was desperately in love with him!

CHAPTER SIX

IT WAS no good wondering how had it happened, or why had it happened. Leith started to come out of her shock to realise it just had! She was up to her ears in love with Naylor Massingham, and there wasn't a single solitary thing she could do about it.

Love, she very swiftly recognised, was a most tormenting emotion, and briefly her thoughts went to Travis, who was so in love and who was having such an awful time of it. Only now, in love herself and with an inner knowledge that nothing could come of that love, could she fully appreciate what Travis was going through. She thought she had been sympathetic to him, but, in the pain of love herself, could she have been kinder?

Thoughts of Travis floated away as thoughts of Naylor pushed him aside. It amazed her, as she stared down at her right hand, that, while loving Naylor with every part of her being, she could have lashed out at him so violently.

Feeling defeated suddenly, she discovered that it was no good trying to recapture the fury she had felt with him in the hope of that fury helping her battle against the way she was feeling. She loved him, and there was no rage in her. This, she realised, was what lay behind that dreadful feeling of alarm she had experienced when Naylor had first stated that she was to be his 'girlfriend'. Her alarm, it was patently obvious to her now, stemmed from a basic instinct of knowing that she was going to end up hurting inside.

This. . . Suddenly, when she had been lost to everything, alarm bells went off again as the sound of someone knocking on her bedroom door penetrated her thoughts. Naylor! It must be him! Yet she didn't want it to be him, she wasn't ready to face him again—not yet. She needed to. . .

Her thoughts ended abruptly as the knock came again, more urgently this time. Leith's thoughts were still suspended in mid-air, when she heard her name called. Travis! Relief washed over her, and she went and opened the door. 'Sorry to be a pest,' Travis apologised, 'but I saw you come back without Naylor,' and while Leith was rapidly trying to find an excuse for her return to the house without the man everyone knew she had gone walking with, she found that Travis was too involved with his own miseries to want to delve into hers, for he went on, 'I've been sitting in the library thinking about Rosemary, and getting more and more uptight about our situation, when you ran in and I started to think about phoning her. You wouldn't, would you?' he asked, his eyes so pleading that Leith, aware that he was asking her to ring Rosemary and then pass the phone over to him, had no thought to refuse.

'Where's the phone?' she asked.

'We can phone from the library, we'll be private in there,' he replied eagerly, his face suddenly alive with excitement.

She went down the stairs with him feeling saddened that, with his parents out, he was so anxious to keep his love for Rosemary a secret that he didn't want Naylor to overhear his telephone conversation.

Travis led the way to the library and, to show that he knew Rosemary's parents' phone number by heart, although he had phoned her there only once, he immediately started to dial. Leith had switched thoughts to

endeavour to find some sound reason for telephoning
Rosemary when he handed the phone over to her.

'Er—hello, Mr Green.' Leith realised she'd better
concentrate hard when she heard Rosemary's father on
the other end. 'It's Leith Everett here. How are you?'

'Quite well, thank you,' was her polite but in no sense
cheerful answer.

'Oh, good,' Leith remarked equally politely. Then,
'May I speak to Rosemary, please?' she asked.

'I'm not sure where she is,' he hedged. 'Shall I take a
message?'

Really! Leith thought crossly, and felt quite annoyed
that Rosemary's father was clearly asking her what she
was calling for. 'I don't mind waiting,' she told him
politely and pleasantly, though she couldn't resist
adding, 'Rosemary and I are friends; I haven't seen her
for ages, so I thought I'd ring up for a chat.'

She flicked a look at Travis as, without so much as
asking her to hold on, Mr Green went away to tell
Rosemary that she was wanted on the phone. Travis was
looking quite downcast, she saw, and she knew the
reason for that. Clearly he had realised that, with Mr
Green answering the phone, any conversation he had
with Rosemary was going to be very one-sided.

'Hello?' Rosemary, sounding quiet and subdued, came
on to the phone.

'Leith here.'

'So my father said.'

'How are things?'

'My mother's much improved.'

Oh, crumbs, Leith thought, and, while knowing
Rosemary to be a highly intelligent girl, had a most
worrying feeling that her parents had been putting some
hard groundwork in on the proposition that, once married, women weren't supposed to have friends!

Fearing then that Rosemary might terminate their

conversation at any moment, she said quickly. 'Travis is here—he wants to have a word.' She heard Rosemary gasp, and promptly passed the phone into his waiting hand.

'Hello, Rosemary,' he began gently, 'I know you can't talk. I just wanted to say hello.'

Leith wondered if she should leave the library, but she did not have to wonder for long. In seconds Travis's conversation with Rosemary was over—and he was looking dreadfully distressed about it.

'It's not fair!' he declared, putting the phone back on its rest. 'She's terrified of them! Lord knows what they say to her, but they must be on at her night and day, to get her into a state where she's afraid to acknowledge me on the phone!'

Leith knew he was bleeding a little inside, but she also knew there wasn't a thing she could say or do to help. 'I'm sorry,' she said simply, and, with a new awareness of how shattering being in love was, she knew something of how very devastated he must be feeling just then.

'It's wicked!' he declared. And, seeming to have a need to talk it all out of his system, 'I know Rosemary loves me, and would divorce her husband if they let her—I just know it. But they—Mr and Mrs Green—by their attitude, are denigrating what's beautiful for me into something sordid. Yet there's nothing sordid to it, so why can't they just accept that Rosemary made a terrible mistake and married a rotter. Surely they can't really want her to pay for that mistake for the rest of her life! It's iniquitous,' he said on a shaky breath, 'that because of them, I can't even tell my own parents—let alone Naylor or Will or Hugo—about my love for her. I tell you, Leith, I'm getting near to the end of my rope!'

'Oh, Travis,' mourned Leith, and, because she felt helpless to give him any verbal comfort, she stretched out a hand of sympathy to his arm.

Her hand was still lightly on his arm when suddenly the library door was pushed inwards. Startled, she jerked her head round, and suddenly wild colour surged into her cheeks. This was the first time she had seen Naylor since her discovery that she loved him. Her heart beat crazily within her as she recalled that the last time she'd seen him she had hit him with all her might—and from the look of fury on his face he was not easily going to forgive her!

She saw his furious glance go to her hand on his cousin's sleeve, and swiftly she dropped her hand to her side. At that same moment, however, Travis, who had appeared equally dumbstruck, seemed to come to and realise that he could no longer continue to speak openly of his love or his problems. Though, since he was still emotionally overwrought, he did the only thing possible.

'See you,' he muttered shakenly, and went quickly towards the door. Naylor stepped to one side, and Travis went hurriedly out of sight.

It seemed an excellent idea to Leith to follow suit. She had got only halfway to the door, however, when Naylor, with no let-up on his fury moved towards her. She moved to one side and so did Naylor. She stood her ground—he came and planted himself in front of her.

Defiantly she looked up at him. She then discovered that she cared not at all for the dangerous glint that suddenly appeared in his eyes as he stared down into her still blush-pinkened skin.

Then furious dark eyes were glaring into hers. 'Let me guess!' he snarled. 'The way you and he have just been pawing each other about just has to mean that, in your own sweet way,' he inserted thunderously, 'you've been endorsing the fact that your affair with him is over!'

'I . . . Y-you. . .' she spluttered, and, loving him, found it absolutely beyond belief that he should believe that she and his cousin had just been having a fine old time. 'Pawing!' she exclaimed, and illogically started to feel angry that this swine of a man she had given her heart to should still be so ready to think the worst of her.

'You're telling me you weren't leading him on?' he challenged toughly, a muscle beating angrily in his temple as, as though striving hard for control, he took an enraged step away. 'That you——'

'I wouldn't dream of telling you anything!' she flared, and as anxiety, love and all manner of emotions flooded her she only knew she had to get away from him. 'If you'll excuse me. . .' she mumbled, and, whether he would or not, she wasn't staying around to find out. Travis had left the door open—she seized her chance, and was through it like a shot.

Reaching her room, she wanted with all her heart to leave Parkwood, and even made a move to get out her overnight bag. But how could she leave when she wanted to be near Naylor? For while she was to some degree confused at that precise moment about the importance of keeping a job that paid well, she knew, whatever else was hazy, that she was very much in love with him.

Leith spent the rest of that afternoon in her room. She heard Mr and Mrs Hepwood return home, and shortly after that felt guilty when Wendy, a sixteen-year-old who helped Mrs Lumsden, the housekeeper, brought a tray of tea up to her.

'I'm to tell you that dinner will be at eight,' Wendy passed the message cheerily.

'Thank you, Wendy.' Leith rose above her inner turmoil to smile her thanks, but was immediately a mass of inner agitation again once Wendy had gone.

Pouring out a cup of tea, she realised that she couldn't very well leave anyway. Good manners, if nothing else, decreed that she stayed. Both Mr and Mrs Hepwood would think it very peculiar if the one and only time their nephew brought one of his female friends home, that female opted to leave without pausing long enough to have dinner.

Restlessly Leith moved over to the window, but while the view from her room was quite exquisite, she saw nothing of it and could see only Naylor's furious face as he accused her of leading Travis on.

It was still very much in her mind as she moved from the window. Then suddenly she stopped dead, realising that, if Naylor thought she hadn't yet completely finished with Travis, then he was just angry enough—and blunt enough—to do it for her.

Quite how he would do that she was undecided when later she ran her bath prior to getting ready to go down to dinner. She hardly thought—since it was plain that Naylor would not want to harm the close bond that existed within the family—that he would bluntly tell Travis to leave her alone. Not that Travis, who wasn't interested in her anyway, would do anything but agree—though Naylor wasn't to know that.

Leith was still puzzling at it when, bathed and dressed in a silky-finish dress of deep amber, she brushed her hair. She had still come to no conclusion about what Naylor would do when, at ten minutes to eight, she left her room.

She went down the stairs and, again remembering Naylor's rage, she was certain about one thing—that, whatever way, whichever way, somehow, if he had not done so already, Naylor would at some time soon take action that would for all time sever the relationship he thought she had with his cousin.

Idiotically, her heart was racing when she reached the drawing-room. She heard the hum of pleasant voices, and guessed she must be last down. She took a steadying breath and went in—and didn't feel steady at all when tall, straight and no-nonsense, Naylor left his chair and came over to her.

'I was about to come looking for you, darling.' He smiled, his eyes taking in her shiny hair, silky dress and everything else about her, and, while Leith was still recovering from the 'darling', he placed a firm, possessive hand on her elbow and guided her into the room.

Darling! Leith still hadn't got herself back together again when the five of them moved to the dining-room. Naylor was up to something, she knew he was; she could almost taste it, so concrete did she feel it. But what?

She did not have to wait very long to find out. The Hepwoods' dining-room, as well as being elegant, had a comfortable air about it. Guthrie Hepwood sat at the head of the table with Leith seated on his right, and with Naylor next to her. Cicely Hepwood sat at the other side of the table next to her husband, with Travis seated next to his mother.

'I've a rather special wine I've been saving for you to sample, Naylor,' Guthrie addressed his nephew as they began to tuck into a starter of scampi in flaky pastry.

'Knowing your superb taste, Uncle, it sounds as if we're in for something of a treat,' Naylor replied. But then, to Leith's surprise, and, from what she could see, everyone else's, he seemed to hesitate. 'Though. . .' he began, and stopped.

All eyes were on him, making it fairly obvious to Leith that his family never saw him hesitate over anything. 'Though?' his uncle queried.

Leith was staring at Naylor too when suddenly he turned to look at her and, to set her heart thundering, smiled, a gentle smile. Then, in the same gentle tone she had heard Travis use when he had been speaking to the woman he loved, he murmured, 'Leith, my darling, I just can't keep it to myself any longer—do you mind?'

'M-m. . .' was as far as she could stammer, for, in the next instant, Naylor was looking past her at his uncle.

'I was rather wondering, Uncle,' he smiled at the man

who had kept a fatherly eye on him from the age of ten, 'how you felt about serving some of that excellent champagne I know you have in your cellar.'

'Champagne?' Guthrie queried, but had the answer from his wife when, with a small squeal of delight, she addressed her nephew.

'Oh, Naylor—you mean. . .?' she gasped.

Leith was looking on, mesmerised, and hardly crediting her hearing as Naylor grinned. 'Yes, Aunt, Leith has this afternoon done me the honour of agreeing to be my wife.'

Agreeing! Wife! Her mouth fell open in shock, but more shock was to come. For, to conceal the fact that in her utter astonishment she was looking ready to drop, Naylor moved his chair closer to her and drew her attention by planting a light and loving kiss on her cheek.

'Leith never said anything about agreeing to marry you when I saw her in the——' Travis left his own unhappy thoughts to start to exclaim.

'Leith is feeling exceedingly shy about it, aren't you, my love?' Naylor butted in, and, staring at him, Leith could see, where no one else could, that he was daring her to contradict him at her peril.

But she had had enough. More than enough! The time had come to end this before it went any further. 'As a matter of fact——' she began—only to have Naylor charmingly take her words from her.

'As a matter of fact,' he sliced in smoothly, 'Leith is career-minded.' While she was absorbing that little gem, 'I never thought I would ever accept a working wife, but,' he paused and gave her a private smile, 'if that's what my darling wants, I just can't stand in the way of her choice to continue working.'

Choice? What choice? Under the cover of the two senior Hepwoods enthusiastically congratulating their

nephew and Guthrie Hepwood taking Travis with him
to his wine cellar to sort through some champagne,
Leith's hate vibes came out with a vengeance.

The meal continued, the champagne was opened,
poured, a toast drunk, and Leith outwardly smiled. The
way she saw it, she could do nothing else, but inwardly
she was boiling with fury. The swine! The devilish,
scheming, clever swine! This, then, was his way of
seeing to it that Travis knew that she was out of bounds.
Not that it would bother Travis one jot. But it bothered
her, because Naylor You'll-do-as-I-say Massingham had
as good as just told her that either she shut up and went
along with everything he said, even to the extent of
pretending to be engaged to him, or he would dismiss
her! Again she felt like getting up and leaving—but to
do that would mean walking out of her job. Her ever-
present enemy, the heavy mortgage she had around her
neck, tripped her up—and she knew she just could not
afford the luxury of following the dictates of her pride.

So she sipped champagne, and smiled, and ate, and all
the while her fury against Naylor simmered away.
Heavens, to think she had actually started to feel *ashamed*
that she had ever hit him! Being dropped head first in an
ants' nest was too good for him!

Leith railed ceaselessly against her 'fiancé' to almost
the very end of the meal. Then suddenly, and sweetly,
she began to realise that, since Travis was no more to
her than a good friend, and she was still going to have
her job at the end of all this, when it finally did end, it
was going to be she who had the last laugh—and not N.
Massingham Esquire.

From then on she started to cheer up.

'Shall we go through to the drawing-room?' her hostess
suggested. Leith made to stand up, and instantly Naylor
was there to pull back her chair.

She looked up at him. Swine, she thought and smiled

lovingly. Then, almost so certain as to be positive that he could not abide a clinging type of woman, she hooked her arm through his. He had brilliant powers of recovery, she realised when, with his look of surprise that she was clinging on to him barely discernible, he placed his hand lovingly over hers. Together they went to the drawing-room.

Together they sat on one of the deep and wide settees in the room, and, though there was room enough to spare should they wish to spread out, Leith opted to sit up close. You want snuggling, I got snuggling, she fumed, knowing for sure that she wasn't the clinging type but, with some devil on her back, this way seeming to be the only way she could cope with being 'engaged'.

That devil forced her to edge up a little nearer to Naylor. He turned his head and smiled down at her—she looked into his eyes, and knew that he wasn't fooled for a minute. 'You're something else again,' he murmured.

'Believe it,' she returned beneath her breath.

'Oh, it's lovely to see you so happy, Naylor!' Cicely Hepwood crooned, and Leith had an unwanted moment of self-disgust that these people were all so happy for Naylor, when everything was just so much sham.

'You certainly live in a splendid spot,' Leith struggled up out of being conscience-stricken to remark.

'We like it,' Guthrie took up. 'We moved here—when was it, Cissy?' he turned to his wife to enquire.

'Twenty-six years ago,' she supplied, shaking her head at his terrible memory. 'Just before Naylor came to live with us.'

'Naylor was ten at the time, wasn't he?' Her own question caught Leith unawares. She hadn't meant to ask anything of the sort, but realised then that her love for Naylor, her basic need to know more and everything about him, had got in the way of the fury she felt at his latest bossy manoeuvre.

'This is a lovely time for you both,' Cicely beamed. 'Naturally you'll have talked and talked endlessly and exchanged details of your life before you knew each other.'

'There has been a bit of that,' Naylor chipped in to own. Then he smiled, as he looked fondly at Leith, and said softly, 'But I'm sure there's a lot about Leith that I've still got to learn.'

'Not at all,' Leith laughed lightly, then found that his aunt, without meaning to pry, she was sure, was asking questions which she must have assumed that Naylor already knew the answers to anyway.

'Do you live in London with your parents, Leith?' she asked interestedly.

Leith saw Travis give her a warning look, but, since Rosemary's name had not so much as been mentioned, much less the name of the place she came from, she saw no harm in revealing, 'My parents live in Dorset.'

'Didn't I hear you mention that you had a brother?' Travis asked before she could reveal anything else about her Dorset connections.

Oh, dear, Leith thought, he's panicking. But, since she'd be hanged if she'd let the man by her side know that the Sebastian of the deerstalker hat was her brother, she left Sebastian's name out of it too. 'That's right,' she smiled. 'But I haven't seen him in simply ages.' She turned back to her hostess to confide, 'My brother's living in India,' and quickly, before anyone could make a meal of that, she laid a possessive hand on Naylor's and queried, 'Did you never think of entering the wine-importing business, darling?'

Oh, my word, she thought, as, though he favoured her with a fond look, the cool calculating gleam in

Naylor's eyes showed he wasn't too impressed to have landed himself such a devoted fiancée.

'I'd have liked Naylor to come into the firm,' Guthrie answered for him. 'Indeed,' he went on, 'I offered him a place in the company. But, as he's no doubt told you, he wouldn't take it.'

'Naylor wouldn't say too much, I expect,' Cicely clipped in warmly. 'He's far too modest.'

'Really, Aunt, you'll have me blushing!' Naylor dropped in lightly.

'That'll be the day,' murmured Leith for his ears alone. 'You're right, of course,' she said generally, 'I know only the barest outline of how he—er. . .' In territory she knew nothing of, she stumbled.

But Guthrie Hepwood was there to take over as, in high good humour, he filled in, 'Naylor's brain works on an instinctive different level from mine—he's a born engineer. It was a foregone conclusion, I soon realised, that after univeristy he'd start up his own firm with some money his father left him. He went from strength to strength,' Guthrie said proudly. 'Of course, he had to work all hours.'

'And still does,' Leith slotted in, easily recalling that the Jaguar was invariably still parked at Vasey's when she left at night.

'I'll change all that when we're married,' Naylor assured her, and her heartbeats raced an erratic rhythm at just the very thought of being married to him.

But cold reality was but a split second away, and Leith went swiftly from dream world to fury that he should involve her in this sham. 'Promises!' she exclaimed on a loving laugh, and thereafter put herself out to be the epitome of all she thought he would most dislike in a woman, shyly calling him darling whenever she had the chance.

There were several times in the next hour when she

would, again with due shyness, look lovingly into his eyes. He bore it all very well, she thought, but by then she was past caring how he was taking it.

It was some time after eleven when noises were made about turning in, though as everyone stood up, to her surprise, though not anyone else's, Travis said he wasn't ready for bed yet and was going out.

'Out—at this time?' his mother protested worriedly.

'Don't fret, there's a love. I promise to return to sleep in my own bed!'

Leith saw Naylor's mouth firm and thought it must be on account of the anxiety that Travis was causing his mother. It could not, by any stretch of the imagination, be because Naylor was remembering another Saturday night when Travis had not slept in his own bed, but a bed Naylor thought was hers.

'Don't make a noise when you come in,' Guthrie warned his son, and Travis uttered his adieux and went on his way.

Cicely put on a cheerful expression and tactfully, as though thinking to leave the newly engaged couple to say goodnight in private, she smiled, 'If you'll excuse us, Leith, Guthrie and I always go and check on the horses before we go up to bed. We've only got two now, but they like us to tell them the details of the day.' Impulsively she came and placed a kiss on Leith's cheek. 'I couldn't be more pleased about you and Naylor,' she said huskily. 'I'm thrilled!'

Leith felt dreadful after her host and hostess had gone, and then more than ever was she furious with Naylor. So furious was she, in fact, that she felt it wiser not to stay in the same room with him. She had hit him at lunchtime—her feelings now were even more murderous.

Without a word she marched from the room. It did

her fury no good at all that Naylor was right there with her when she reached the stairs.

'You know, of course, that Travis has gone to get plastered,' he charged aggressively as they started up the stairs.

'That's my fault, naturally!' she snapped, not halting in her step, but knowing that if Travis had gone to get plastered, as was probably true, it was not on account of her.

'Whose fault would it be but yours?' Naylor snarled as they reached the landing. 'You've been making a meal of me with your eyes all evening!'

'Look here, *you!*' Leith exploded as, having walked smartly along the landing, she halted at her bedroom door. 'It was *you*, not me, who announced that we were engaged. It was *you*, when I was ready to deny any such ridiculous notion, who threatened me with the loss of my job if I didn't back you up all the way! It was——'

'Well, you sure as hell backed me up!' he grated, hell-bent on a fight, she would swear; something was eating away at him anyway. 'My stars, did you come across as eager! You. . .' Suddenly he halted, and aggression such as she'd never seen before filled him. 'Hell's teeth,' he ground out, 'were you as clinging with him as you were with me?'

Aggression or no aggression, Leith had had a surfeit of him and his calling the shots. Furiously she opened her bedroom door and, flicking the light on, went in, then turned to serve him a final volley before she slammed the door shut in his face. 'Clinging?' she snapped. 'You know better than most, Naylor, that there were *some* nights when I couldn't bear to let him go home at all!'

She had her hand on the door, but, before she could follow through her intention to slam it in his face, Naylor gave a mighty roar of utter outrage. The next Leith knew, he had crashed the door furiously back on its hinges and was coming forward.

Fear gripped her at the demoniacal glint in his dark eyes. That fear did not abate when, briefly, he halted. For he halted only to slam the door fast behind him, then, having imprisoned her in her room, he was again coming after her.

'Get out!' she yelled while she still had breath, but, even as she started backing rapidly, she knew he had no intention whatsoever of obeying her orders. 'Leave me alone!' she screamed when her efforts to evade him proved useless and a pair of iron hands fastened on her arms.

'Like hell I will, sweetheart!' he snarled savagely. 'You've been asking for this all night!'

In the next second his arms were iron bands around her, and he was seeking and finding her mouth. Her lips parted in protest; he seemed to enjoy their shape. 'No!' she shrieked, and managed a half-turn away from him, then discovered that he had found a way of keeping her exactly where he wanted her. For a brief moment later, he had picked her bodily up in his arms, and, as if she weighed less than nothing, was carrying her over to the bed. 'No! No!' she shrieked, but found she was wasting her breath.

Then she found that she had no breath, for all the breath went out of her body when he tossed her down on to her mattress. She discovered she was a split second too late in making a hurried scramble to get off the bed, because, in the next instant, Naylor was there with her, pinning her down with his body.

'Now give me the big come-on with those gorgeous green orbs,' he gritted.

'Go to hell!' she shouted, and didn't at all like the smile that crossed his features.

'I very probably will, but not before I've taken you!' he gritted.

Oh, heavens, Leith thought, trying her hardest to keep a lid on her panic. 'Y-you—you—intend to rape me?' she cried jerkily.

'Rape, *darling*,' he sneered, 'never entered my head.'

'Then you might as well let me get up right now!' she retorted while her courage held her out.

'You're saying that rape is the only way I'm going to make you mine?' he questioned, and, to make her treacherous body betray her, he planted a spine-thrilling kiss on the side of her throat.

'That's what I'm saying,' she told him chokily, and felt more treachery from her body as he placed his warm mouth over hers and kissed her long and lingeringly. Her nails were biting into her palms when he pulled back and looked down into her face.

'Who are you trying to kid?' he taunted, and somehow he seemed to know, though how she didn't know, that she had been within an ace of responding to him.

Leith swallowed hard, and knew, before the weakness of loving him, the weakness of wanting him battered down the rest of her defences, small though those defences were, that she had to appeal to that in him which she somehow knew would make him hate himself if he took her.

His head came down again, and suddenly, as her whole body started to come alive, Leith found she was having to fight herself as well as him. 'Please, Naylor!' she erupted on a panicky breath, and, when he hesitated and stared into her alarmed green eyes, 'Please d-don't,' she stammered.

'Give me one good reason,' he demanded, somehow his voice reaching her as gruff and as if he was under some powerful emotion too.

'I'm—I'm—a virgin,' she told him honestly, and saw

him move involuntarily as though startled, as though that had never occurred to him. But she at once saw that he was immediately discounting it.

'You might have been once, but not since you were about seventeen, I'll bet,' he gritted, and his head came down.

'No!' she protested when that kiss broke.

'Oh, but yes, my lovely,' he crooned silkily, and suddenly, as his head came down again, the time for talking was over.

Inside thirty seconds Leith was lost. Another thirty seconds went by, during which time Naylor traced kisses down her throat and to the neck of her dress, and Leith was struggling to get her hands free—so she could wrap her arms around him.

Time meant nothing then when kiss after kiss they shared, and, as Naylor pressed her to the mattress, Leith pressed closer to him.

His kisses had gentled out when suddenly, while still staying on the mattress with her, he moved away from her. But she didn't want him even that far away, and in a mindless vortex of wanting, she, who she knew for certain was not the clinging type, clung on to him. Then she felt his fingers at the zip of her dress, and breathed a sigh of relief. Naylor wasn't rejecting her—he just wanted to get closer to her.

She felt gloriously unashamed when, with her outer covering in a silken heap on the floor, he took her in his arms once more. 'Beautiful Leith,' he murmured, and buried his face in her luxurious chestnut mane.

'Naylor,' she whispered, and knew yet more rapture when his mouth returned to take her lips while his warm and gentle hands caressed in sensual, skin-tingling movement from her throat, over her shoulders, down to her waist, and then, in a wonderful touch, upwards to capture her breasts. 'Naylor!' she sighed again in the utmost rapture, and, clutching him, had not the smallest demur to make when he removed her bra and began to caress the swollen mounds of her pink-tipped breasts.

A convulsive feeling took her, and she wasn't sure she hadn't called his name again. What she was sure of, though, was that she wanted him with every fibre of her being. More, she had to tell him so.

'I want you,' she cried, and loved him. 'Oh, Naylor,' she cried in her inexperience, 'I want you so!'

'Wait, my lovely,' he breathed, and took his eyes from her wanting, flushed face, to pull back and stare as though transfixed at the throbbing globes of her breasts. He stretched out and long sensitive fingers caressed the hardened peaks. 'You're exquisite, Leith,' he said softly, 'so exquisite,' and, as if her beauty was too much for him to bear, he closed his eyes.

Suddenly the sound of a door, of someone coming in from outside, brought Leith tumbling, falling back down to earth. Though afterwards she was fairly certain that Naylor had always meant to reject her anyway. But at that moment, as Cicely and Guthrie Hepwood came back into the house from the stables, all she knew was that, while she still wanted Naylor, she could not let him make love to her—not in his aunt's and uncle's house with them only in the next-door room, for all she knew.

Though had Leith any anxieties about telling him of her feelings, then she discovered that they were unnecessary anyway, for, glancing at Naylor again, she saw that a cold mask seemed to have slipped over his features. Abruptly he sat up, away from her, and Leith knew he had gone off any idea of making love to her.

When he bent to the floor and picked up her dress and draped it anyhow over her, though making sure that her breasts, which he had just termed 'exquisite', were covered, she knew he was very much off *her* too. And that was before, halfway to the door, he turned and flicked a glance at her still flushed face, then fired, sarcastically, cruelly, 'With regard to your being a virgin, sweetheart, I'll bet you say that to all your lovers!'

Leith rolled over and buried her head in her pillow the moment the door had closed. While hating him she had loved him, and, loving him, had no shame in wanting him to be her only mate.

But shame was there in vast amounts as, sleepless, she waited for the night to pass. She had known they weren't going to make love the moment the sound of that door being either opened or closed had penetrated, and flooding in had come the memory that she was Mr and Mrs Hepwood's guest. But did the man she had wanted to lie with have to be such a swine—and make out that she was just anybody's?

Leith finally drifted off into a troubled sleep, wondering if there was any greater torment than that of loving unwisely.

CHAPTER SEVEN

AFTER a wretched night Leith was up early on Sunday, was bathed and dressed and wanting, with all she had, to be back home in her London apartment.

When later she left her room, while feeling agitation and a mixture of disturbed pride and discomposure about seeing Naylor again, she anticipated that it would be another six hours before they left Parkwood.

He was in the drawing-room with his uncle when she went in. She saw Naylor's sharp glance go over her, but, while she quickly lowered her glance, she could do nothing about the unexpected riot of colour that flooded her face.

Her complexion was still a heightened pink when Naylor left his uncle and came over to her. She raised her eyes, saw his glance rake over her face, and was certain he was discounting entirely that her blush could have anything to do with the fact that, after being nearly naked in his arms, she was feeling a trifle uncomfortable at seeing him again. Whatever, it was plain he did not like it.

Though, ever a man to confuse her, he greeted her pleasantly, 'Good morning, darling,' and, in case she hadn't got the message that the endearment was only on account of their audience, 'I've just been telling my uncle that we'll be leaving after breakfast.'

Conversely, when that was just what she wanted, suddenly Leith felt alarm that her weekend with Naylor would so soon be over. Being in love, she was realising, made a complete and utter nonsense of everything.

'Are you sure you have to go so soon?' Cicely protested over breakfast.

'I wish we could stay, Aunt,' Naylor replied charmingly, and took her mind away from him by asking, 'Did Travis come home last night?'

'Oh, yes,' she answered lightly, and turning to Leith, 'I'm afraid Travis doesn't always surface to join us for breakfast on Sunday morning.'

Leith smiled pleasantly, but on turning her head she suddenly met Naylor's gaze full on. The look in his eyes was cool and lofty, she saw, and she just knew then that he was thinking that there were some Sundays when Travis breakfasted at someone else's table—and he knew exactly where!

So she was not feeling at all friendly to Naylor when, shortly after breakfast, they left Parkwood. From the lack of conversation on the way back to her flat, she rather gathered that she wasn't Naylor Massingham's favourite person either.

Which suited her fine. Though, had she thought she might get out of his car and leave him without so much as a word being said between them, she found she was mistaken.

She did get out of his car without a word when he stopped it outside her address—but so did he. She looked at him, then realised her overnight bag was in the boot. She walked round to the rear of the car and stood silently while he undid the boot and picked up her bag.

'Leith,' he said, but his look was no warmer, no less arrogant than it had been all morning, 'you don't. . .' he went on, and seemed slightly stuck for words.

But she wasn't waiting around to hear the rest of it. 'That's true, I don't!' she snapped, and, yanking her overnight bag out of his hands, she turned and marched smartly indoors.

That Sunday seemed to go on forever. Alternately

loving and hating, Leith just couldn't get Naylor out of her mind. His 'Leith, you don't. . .' couldn't have been very important either, otherwise, knowing him, he'd have charged after her and made her listen.

When eventually she left the sitting-room to go to bed, she pattered into the hall, knowing in advance that she was in for another wretched night of it. Suddenly, though, as her glance went without her really seeing, over the coat-and-hat fitment, she was jolted to a standstill. Where was Sebastian's hat? She searched for it, thought it might have fallen down, but could find it nowhere!

'And get rid of that!' she clearly recalled hearing Naylor tell her—in fact, the way he'd bellowed out the order, it wouldn't surprise her if the whole avenue hadn't heard it. Yet he wouldn't, would he?

Leith went to bed and could see no other answer. She had put Sebastian's hat back where it belonged, and it had still been there yesterday morning before Naylor had called for her. So, unless she'd had burglars—and nothing else had been taken—then Naylor, not caring to have his orders disobeyed, must have removed it.

For one crazy, idiotic moment, Leith thought Naylor might have disposed of Sebastian's deerstalker because it caused him some small degree of jealousy to see another man's hat in her home. That thought did not stay around long. All too soon she realised how howlingly ridiculous such a notion was. The only reason Naylor had removed that hat was that he had ordered her to do it and, unused to not being obeyed, had taken it upon himself to remove it personally—no argument.

It took her an absolute age to get off to sleep that night, and what sleep she did get was only sketchy. Consequently she was having her first decent sleep in a couple of nights when her alarm clock went off the next morning. She slept right through it. When an hour later she did surface, she knew at once that there was no way she was going to make it to the office on time.

She showered, dressed and snatched a cup of coffee on hurried auto-pilot, and was in her car on her way to her place of employment without any clear recollection of having done any of the three.

She raced inside the Vasey building and congratulated herself that she had caught up time, and was now only half an hour late. She began to relax a little as she neared the department where she worked, then realised that any vague notion that she might slip into her office without anyone noticing was a non-starter—everybody seemed to be looking at her!

Oh, dear, she thought, half an hour late, and I get a persecution complex—of course people weren't staring at her.

'Wow!' Paul Fisher exclaimed as she went quickly past him, but his 'wow' meant nothing to her other than that, unfortunately, his carpeting of a week last Friday had had no lasting effect.

'Sorry to be late,' she told Jimmy when she made it to her own office. 'Have there been any——' She broke off when it dawned on her that Jimmy was staring at her. 'What. . .?' she began.

'When you weren't here at nine, I thought maybe you wouldn't be coming in again,' Jimmy remarked, and, before she could ask him what he meant by that, 'I like your hair that way, Leith,' he opined.

Instinctively she put a hand to her hair. Only then did she realise that, her actions automatic that morning, she had forgotten to scrape her hair back in its comparatively recent workday knot. Nor, she realised, did she have her glasses on. 'Thanks,' she muttered, but had no time at all in which to decide if she should nip to the cloakroom and get to work with her comb, for Jimmy's next remarks were to have her reeling—and furious.

'You've had a visitor, by the way,' he announced cheerfully. 'He didn't leave his name, but he said he'd call back.' Then, while Leith was wondering which stranger to Jimmy from which department had called in her absence, his cheerful face was splitting from ear to ear as he asked, 'Do I congratulate you or your fiancé?' And, while she was staring at him thunderstruck, 'I never know whether it's the man you congratulate or the woman, but anyway, I'm dead chuffed about your engagement.' Leith still hadn't found her voice. 'We all are!' he beamed.

'All?' she gasped.

'You never expected the news of your engagement to Mr Massingham to stay a secret for long, did you?' Jimmy crowed. 'Everybody knows. I——' The ringing of the telephone cut him off, and as he went to answer it Leith, while coping with shock, began to get furious. 'It's for you,' Jimmy told her, and, when she shook her head, nowhere near ready yet to cope with her job, he mouthed, 'It's Mr Massingham.'

Leith took the phone from him. 'Yes?' she said into the mouthpiece.

'My office—*now!*' Bang, the phone went down. Very lover-like, I'm sure! Leith fumed.

'Mr Massingham wants to see me,' she told Jimmy on her way out.

'Looking the way you do, I'll bet he does!' Jimmy grinned—at any other time Leith might have had a quiet word with him about his cheek. Just then she had other things on her mind.

She had to run the barrage of more glances as she made her way over to the new extension, but she knew then that people looking at her was not on account of her being half an hour late, but on account of everyone, it seemed, knowing of her engagement. Vasey's, like any other establishment, was a hotbed of gossip. Though the

news of her 'engagement' could not possibly have come
from any other source than he of the 'My office—*now*'
order.

He hadn't sounded very pleased about something—
that made two of them. She wasn't very pleased either.
How could he let it be known to all and sundry that they
were 'engaged'—how *could* he?

'Go straight in!' Moira Russell exclaimed when, not
pausing in her stride, Leith banged in through her office
door and kept going in the direction of the other door in
the room.

'Thanks!' Leith threw over her shoulder in passing,
and without pausing to knock she opened the door on
her stride and went 'straight in'.

Naylor was standing by his desk. Leith closed the
door with an angry thud, then opened her mouth to let
fly—but he got in first.

'What the *hell* sort of game do you think you're
playing?' he snarled.

'*Me*?' Leith wasted not another second. 'How *dare* you
announce——?'

'You know damn well our 'engagement' was only for
family consumption! You——'

'Who in creation do you think——?'

'Well, take it from me, lady,' his aggression was in
full force, 'no one gets their hooks into me that——'

Hooks! 'You think that I. . .!' Utterly flabbergasted,
Leith began to realise that *he* was accusing *her* of
announcing their 'engagement' to all and sundry. 'I
haven't breathed a. . .' She broke off, and could see
from his arrogant aggressive stance that she could deny
his accusation until she was blue in the face but he was
not going to believe her. 'Hooks into you!' she scorned.
'Ye gods, Massingham,' she went on, covering like fury
the fact that he could hurt without even trying, 'my
memory is vivid that *that* great a lover you're not!'

Oh, oh, her lie bounced off him, but he didn't like her arrogance one little bit, she could tell. All the same, she was totally unprepared for the double helping of hurt he dished out next. 'Since you remember those moments we shared so *vividly*, my prowess as a lover must have left some impression on you,' he gritted toughly, then, his eyes glinting dangerously, he told her, straight from the shoulder, 'Though in actual fact I wasn't talking of our time on your bed, but of your interest in my financial standing!'

'Oh!' she gasped, and unable to believe that he should think such a thing, let alone say it, she was not sure she did not lose some of her colour. Abruptly she spun round, needing to go, needing to hide her hurt.

But he'd seen her hurt, she realised, for even as she made a dash for the door, he caught up with her and, to her astonishment, there was not a scrap of aggression in him as he groaned, 'Oh, lord,' and more astonishingly, he gently put his arms around her.

He didn't apologise for what he'd just said, she didn't expect him to. But then, as she stood stiff and resisting in his arms, he suddenly applied a gentle pressure, and all at once she was against his chest. She held out for a mammoth ten seconds and then, weak where he was concerned, she could hold out no longer, and collapsed weakly, clingingly, against him.

He did not kiss her, she did not want him to. She knew that soon she would come to her senses, but for now it was just sheer bliss to be here, up against his heart.

'You're wearing your hair down,' he murmured from somewhere above her head.

'I overslept and f-forgot to pin it back in my rush,' she told him openly.

'I—like it,' he breathed, and she wasn't at all certain then that he didn't kiss the top of her head.

Oh, how she loved him! She had loved him while hating him, had loved him when he'd been a perfect swine. But oh, how much she loved him when he held her to his heart, and was gentle, like now.

I'm going delirious, she thought, and knew she should be making an effort to get herself back together again. Striving hard for some normality, she pulled her head back and told him, 'I d-didn't say a word to anyone about—about us.'

Her heart was racing like an express train as she saw that the look in his eyes was as gentle as his hold, as he told her, 'Neither did I!' They stood like that, looking into each other's eyes, when the door opened. 'So who——?' he began, and they both turned, aware that they were not alone.

'Travis!' Leith exclaimed, though she realised she should not have been so surprised. What was more natural than that he should come to see his cousin at his place of work?

'Hello, Leith—Naylor.' Travis smiled, and as Leith suddenly realised how she and Naylor with their arms about each other must look to anyone coming in, self-conscious all of a sudden, she stepped out of Naylor's hold. Not that he tried to hold on to her and not that Travis appeared to think there was anything out of the way in the two of them embracing—she gathered she had their engagement to thank for that. Then she discovered that it was Travis she had to thank that the news of her engagement to his cousin was all over Vasey's, as, still smiling, he stated, 'Hope you don't mind, Naylor, but I came in earlier to have a quick word with Leith, and couldn't resist telling her assistant that a possible reason for Leith being late this morning could be her getting engaged to you at the weekend.'

Leith was overwhelmingly aware of Naylor's speculative glance at both her and Travis—and knew the reason for it. For someone who, according to Naylor's belief, should be sorely upset that the woman he loved was engaged to another, Travis was coping exceedingly well.

She thought, since Naylor now knew that she wasn't the one responsible for 'advertising' their 'engagement'—which had clearly been the reason for his 'My office—*now*!' command—that now might be as good a moment as any to leave. 'I'd better get back and get some work done,' she said to anybody who was interested.

'I must get a move on too,' declared Travis, and while he delayed to exchange one or two pleasantries with his cousin, Leith hotfooted it out of there. She was going along one of the corridors when Travis caught up with her. 'I had to come especially to see you this morning, Leith,' he said earnestly as he fell into step with her.

'Rosemary?' she guessed.

'For once, not Rosemary, though I'm getting more and more desperate about not knowing what to do for the best,' he confessed, but went on to explain, 'I spent a lot of time yesterday in realising that I must have been a real wet blanket when Naylor announced your engagement on Saturday.'

'You weren't,' Leith assured him, but, while she wanted to tell him that she and Naylor were not engaged—or ever likely to be—she somehow found she couldn't.

But Travis was shaking his head, and insisting that he had not been as enthusiastic as he might have been on Saturday. 'After all you've done in the past for Rosemary and me, and are still doing,' he went on, 'I got to thinking yesterday that I could have been a sight more energetic in letting you know how delighted I am that you're going to marry my cousin. Which is why I made up my mind to come and tell you first thing that I couldn't think of anyone I'd rather Naylor married.'

'Oh, Travis,' Leith said helplessly.

'You hadn't arrived when first I came,' he went on, 'so I went out and had a coffee, and when I came back your assistant told me you were with Naylor.'

Again Leith wanted to tell him he could forget all idea of her ultimately becoming his cousin by marriage, but again, she found she could not. 'You're sweet,' she said simply, knowing then that because his lack of enthusiasm on Saturday had worried him, he had determined to see her in person that morning.

A few minutes later she parted from him and, weathering a few pleasant glances, went back to her office. She was uncertain whether, at work, she should be denying the rumour that she was engaged to the head of the Massingham empire, but thought that if Naylor had any strong views on the subject she'd soon be hearing about them anyway. Though since, should he do nothing, then in the way of all these things the news would only be a nine-days' wonder, she had other matters to concentrate on.

Chief among those other matters, though, was the speculative way Naylor had looked at her and Travis in his office. She felt certain then that whether Naylor called her back to the new extension to tell her to deny that she was engaged to him or not, she would without fail, before five o'clock that day, be summoned to account for Travis's unexpected easy acceptance of her getting engaged to someone else.

When five o'clock came, however, and not one word had she heard from Naylor, Leith, with something akin to relief, realised that she had been mistaken. She left her office at about five forty-five, saw Naylor's Jaguar in the car park and went weak at the knees about him for a few seconds, then she determinedly got into her own car and drove home.

While making herself a light meal, though, she found

she couldn't stop dreaming about him. He'd been so gentle that morning when he must have seen he had hurt her feelings, and she felt good inside that she had seen the more gentle, considerate side of him. Given that he had half frightened her to death to begin with, he'd been a gentle lover too, she recalled, a tender smile playing around her mouth. There was a wealth of passion in him, but whether—perhaps because of her very limited experience in these matters—something of her shyness had communicated itself to him or not, he had seemed to temper his passion, for the moment, to suit hers.

With her thoughts going dreamily round and round, it was about seven-thirty that, as she was again thinking of how he had that morning cradled her so gently when he'd seen her hurt, Leith suddenly became horror-struck. Oh, dear heavens, had Naylor, by seeing she was hurt, seen too that she cared deeply for him?

Leith spent the next few minutes in a panic. She thought then that she could take anything but that he should know she loved him. When another few minutes went by she was scratching her head to try and think up some way of making sure that Naylor would consider any such notion laughable.

She had still not come up with anything brilliant when ten minutes later someone rang her doorbell fairly aggressively. She had waited all day for Naylor to send for her—by the sound of it, the confrontation was to be on her property, not his.

She went to answer her door, and just knew it would be him. Her heart was racing before she pulled the door open. It gave another spurt of energy to see the tall man she loved standing there.

'Come in,' she invited, knowing full well that he had no intention of delivering any of his remarks from where he stood anyhow.

Leading the way to her sitting-room, she turned to

face him, and saw that any gentleness of expression was long since a thing of the past. The aggression she was more familiar with back in place when, entirely without preamble, he demanded, 'What did Travis want "a quick word" with you about?'

'What would he want a word about?' she questioned hostilely, wanting him to be gentle as he had been that morning. 'He wanted to have a word with me about our engagement—yours and mine, that is.'

'It's as sure as hell you're not getting engaged to him!' he grated.

'So you tell me!' he snapped.

'You have other ideas?'

'Would I dare?'

'Not if you want to keep your job!' he snarled, and, on the brink of all-out warfare, 'Do you have some secret understanding with him that I know nothing of?'

'How do you mean?' The only secret she had with Travis was about Rosemary, but, since Naylor had never heard of Rosemary, he couldn't have sensed that Travis had lost his heart to her neighbour, could he?

'How else would I mean? Are you two-timing me?'

From the jut of his chin if nothing else, Leith knew that woe betide her if she was. 'I know your opinion of *me* is less than nothing, but do you truly think your cousin would continue to be my—er—lover, now that he knows I'm engaged to you?'

Naylor tossed her a look of dislike. 'So you've finished with him?' he calculated.

Leith drew a shaky breath and was about to give Naylor the straightforward 'yes' that he wanted. Then suddenly, while aware she had told him that she did not love Travis, she realised that here was her chance of clouding the issue of who it was that she did love. 'I've—finished with him, yes,' she told him stiffly, 'but only now do I realise that Travis will always be someone special for me.'

The look of intense dislike Naylor sent her at her answer seared right through her. 'So long as it doesn't interfere with your work!' he snarled, and, as if he could no longer bear to be in the same room with her, he turned and strode from her sitting-room, through her hall, and out of her flat.

Leith sank down into a chair the moment the outer door had closed behind him and discovered that she was trembling. So much dislike, when she loved him so much—it was hard to take.

She did not sleep well again that night, though with Naylor so much in her thoughts she had hardly expected to. Again and again in the night hours she thought of him, of his aggression and of the barely veiled hint in his parting shot 'so long as it doesn't interfere with your work!' that for all she had, so far, gone along with everything he had decreed, she could still find herself out of a job if she didn't toe the line.

On that unhappy note she fell asleep, but the next time she awoke—to the clamouring of her alarm clock— she woke up in more ways than one. For suddenly she knew what she had to do.

She got out of bed and thought everything over very carefully, and although it was difficult to keep emotion out of it, she still came back to the self-same answer. She must leave Vasey's.

She drove herself to work and could still see nothing else for it. True, she was going to leave herself with one very big headache with regard to her mortgage, but even that was not unsurmountable. For, according to the terms of her contract with Vasey's, with the exception of a clause giving them the right to instant dismissal should she ever be guilty of industrial misconduct, either party was to give the other three months' notice. In three months, if all went well, she would be out of her flat with a tenant supplying the funds to pay the mortgage. In three months, too, while she knew she wouldn't get a job that paid as well as the one she had now, she should have secured another job, shouldn't she?

She sent Jimmy off on an errand as soon as she got in, then sat down and wrote out her notice. She knew it was going to hurt like crazy giving up her chances of ever catching a glimpse of Naylor again, but she knew in her heart of hearts that the action she was taking was the only one possible. She couldn't take any more of Naylor's aggression, of Naylor looking at her with such dislike, of Naylor thinking she was anybody's. But, most of all, she couldn't take the risk of Naylor guessing, from some thoughtless word or look, that she thought the world of him.

'I'm going to Mr Drewer's office,' she told Jimmy when he came back, and taking the envelope with her resignation in with her, she went to see her head of department.

'Mr Drewer's out for a few minutes—can I help?' his secretary asked.

'Will you give him this?' Leith requested, and went back to her own office, where for the next twenty minutes she tried to pick up the threads of her job.

Her concentration was still not one hundred per cent, though, when suddenly, forcefully, and to make her spin round in surprise, someone burst into her office.

Alarm brought her to her feet as Naylor Massingham instructed Jimmy unceremoniously, '*Out!*'

'Yes, sir!' Jimmy replied quickly, and went, like a bat out of hell.

'I've just been speaking to Drewer,' rapped Naylor. 'When, in answer to his assumption that there was to be an early wedding, I asked what was going round the grapevine now, he told me it was pure speculation on his part, stemming from the fact that you'd just handed in your resignation.' Leith could see at once that he didn't seem to be too enamoured that she, by giving in her notice, had just taken away his trump card. But she was entirely unprepared for the utter pugnacity of him when he snarled harshly, 'So tell me, Miss Everett, just what in thunder do you mean by thinking you're going to leave!'

'You can't stop me leaving!' she erupted defensively. 'I've every——'

'I can't stop you leaving, true,' he agreed furiously, 'But I sure as hell can stop you getting work in your present occupation!'

Leith gasped, then stared at him disbelievingly. 'You—*wouldn't*?' she uttered in shocked tones.

'Try me!' he rapped. 'A phone call, a word dropped into the right ear about how you fouled up the Norwood & Chambers contract. . .' He had no need to go on.

But Leith just could not believe it. Though when, clearly a man who felt he had no need to underline anything, by his very silence he made her believe it, she was back to hating him with a vengeance.

'You *bastard*!' she hissed.

He was undented—and undeterred. 'Happy engagement to you, too, sweetheart!' he fired.

CHAPTER EIGHT

SOMEHOW Leith got through Wednesday and Thursday, but when she drove to work on Friday she was still uncertain whether she would be leaving Vasey's in three months' time or not. She owned that she was feeling too despondent to look for another job, and knew that that despondency stemmed from the fact that she knew she would stand little chance of getting the sort of work she wanted anyhow. It was certain that any future employer would be bound to write to Vasey's for a reference, and, since she didn't doubt for a minute that Naylor had helped himself to her personnel file and, equally without doubt, had instructed Personnel to contact him with any matter pertaining to his 'fiancée', he was in a prime situation to block her application.

Parking her car, Leith supposed she *was* still 'engaged' to him. She had neither seen nor heard him since he'd as good as thrown Jimmy out of the office on Tuesday morning, and started laying down the law.

'Morning, Jimmy!' she greeted her assistant cheerfully, not wanting to give him an inch from which he could make a yard.

'Good morning, Leith,' he answered, and commented seriously, 'I really, really do like your hair done that way.'

Because it suddenly seemed idiotic to go back to wearing her hair in an unbecoming knot, Leith, besides dispensing with her glasses, had reverted to her old hairstyle. But, from the calf-eyed way Jimmy was now looking at her, the last thing she needed just then was that he should go and get a crush on her.

'Thanks,' she told him briefly. 'Now, where shall we start?'

They thereafter worked solidly until just after eleven, when he went off for a coffee and a chat with whoever was near the coffee dispenser. Leith worked on for a few minutes, then realised that she wanted some information from one of the other offices.

She had better things to do than to wait for Jimmy to return, and was halfway up a corridor when, to make her pulse beat faster, she saw Naylor coming from the opposite direction.

What he was doing in her section she neither knew nor cared. All she cared about just then was keeping her composure. Luckily, there was no one else about, or she might have had to stop for the look of the thing—presuming she was still affianced to him. As it was, knowing he would have had to be blind not to see her since they would pass within two feet of each other, and since she had nothing that she wanted to say to him, she opted to walk by him without a word. To show how much he cared, she could have been any one of his minions for all the notice he took of her.

Everything about her errand went from her head once he had gone past, and finding that she felt all over the place just from seeing him, so close, yet so far apart, she ducked into the nearest cloakroom to try to get herself more of one piece.

When she returned to her office she discovered that Jimmy had brought her a coffee—and that she was without the information she had originally set out to get. 'Jimmy. . .' she began.

By four that afternoon Leith was still thinking it utterly astonishing that just seeing Naylor, without so much as exchanging one word, either pleasant or unpleasant, should have left her in such a state. Then the phone rang.

'I think it's Mr Massingham,' was all Jimmy said in an urgent whisper as he passed the phone over to her. On the instant, Leith was again feeling just like jelly inside.

'Hello,' she said down the phone, and was gripping it hard when Jimmy was proved right.

'I should like to see you,' Naylor said coolly, evenly, and without aggression. Leith knew, however, that that meant nothing.

'Now?' she queried, while wondering how the dickens her suddenly shaky legs were going to get her anywhere.

'Why not?' he replied, and quietly put the phone down.

My word, we're coming on! Leith thought, remembering the way he had banged the phone down in her ear the last time. 'I—er—shouldn't be long,' she told Jimmy. 'I'm——'

'Going to the new extension.'

'You're too bright for this place,' she somehow managed to mutter drily.

She was a mass of uneasiness as she left her office and made her way through the corridors, and her thoughts darted in many directions as she tried to fathom why Naylor should want to see her, though, since he was a law unto himself, she realised it was anybody's guess.

He wouldn't ask her to his office in order to give her a verbal tongue-lashing for ignoring him when they'd passed each other in that corridor that morning, would he? she wondered as she reached Moira Russell's door. Since he had ignored her in return, she didn't think he could be that unfair, she considered as she went in.

'Mr Massingham *is* free,' Moira Russell smiled.

'Thanks,' Leith smiled back, and hoped her smile hid the all-over-the-place way she was feeling inside as she crossed the carpet, knocked on Naylor's door, took a quick breath, and went in.

Naylor was not seated at his desk, but was standing, some papers in his hand. Leith's heart turned over—oh, dear heaven, how much she loved him! 'Hello,' some actress deep within her greeted him breezily for his secretary's benefit. Then, as his glance flicked over her, she closed the door. 'You wanted to see me?'

'Come in,' he invited her further into the room, then, dropping the papers down on his desk, he walked away from her, to go and take a look out of the window. He was silent for some seconds, as though what he could see from the window was of much interest. Then all at once he abruptly left his contemplations and looked swiftly and directly over at her, to state, 'Apparently my aunt and uncle are exceedingly keen to get to know the woman I'm going to marry.' Leith stared at him, and while she felt a stab of pain that, whoever Naylor married, it would not be her, he added smoothly, 'They'd like us both to join them at Parkwood for the weekend.'

No! screamed her head, she'd had enough. 'For a start,' she began to voice her objection, 'I'm not going to marry you, and. . .' Her voice faded when she saw the way a muscle throbbed in his temple, and saw his head jerk back, then saw from his sudden glower that she seemed to have offended him in some way.

It took but a moment, though, for her to realise that she hadn't so much offended him as irritated him with her presumption. For his tone was icy as he blasted her cuttingly, 'You might wait until you're asked before you refuse!' Surprisingly, however, while Leith was inwardly wincing at so being put in her place, and thinking that she'd be damned if she'd go with him to Parkwood ever again, it was just as if he had read her hurt, her mutiny, because suddenly his tone was less harsh, as he told her, 'My aunt and uncle have been like parents to me—I owe them a lot.'

'Does that include lying to them?' she snapped, to

counteract that the softening in his tone, his confidences
about his personal life, were going to make her feel
absurdly weak where he was concerned.

'You know why I had to lie to them!' he retaliated, his
softer tone soon gone.

'Refresh my memory!'

'You need reminding that I took you to their home
last weekend in order to show Travis that you—"love"
another!' His 'love' another—himself, in fact—was
much too close for comfort. Instinctively, Leith turned
to the door, ready to get out of there. 'I could dismiss
you on the spot!' Naylor exploded, before she could
move a step.

She stood stock still, then, feeling she had got herself
more under control, she slowly turned. It went without
saying that, even if she took him to any tribunal for
unfair dismissal—not that she could see herself doing
that—he'd probably win hands down. So there was a
fair degree of hate in her eyes as she questioned hostilely,
'Without pay, of course?' too late realising that she had
just given away the fact that she had no reserves of
savings to fall back on.

'Damn right!' he tossed at her unequivocally.

'Damn *you*!' Leith let fly.

Naylor shrugged, careless of her fury, her feelings.
'Whatever,' he barked, 'until I say differently, you're
still my fiancée.' And, having delivered that statement,
'I'll pick you up at eleven tomorrow.'

Leith stared rebelliously at him for about three seconds, then, as fate laughed hollowly at her puny assertion
that she would never again go to Parkwood, she turned
and hurried away from him.

She was still smarting from his bossy treatment of her
when she went home, and spent the whole evening
wondering why she hadn't told him to go to the devil,
dismiss her, and be done with it.

By morning she didn't know where she was anyway. It seemed to her then that there was absolutely no logic in any of it. Oh, she was aware that she had to keep quiet about Rosemary being Travis's girlfriend and not her, but why in creation was she going to Parkwood this weekend?

She bathed and dressed in a linen two-piece, and didn't like any better this Saturday than she had last Saturday to think that in order that Travis should cease to think of her as his girlfriend—something he never had done anyhow—she was going to his home with Naylor. The only difference this Saturday was that this time she was going, not just as Naylor's girlfriend, but his fiancée! So where was the logic in Naylor taking her to Parkwood so that his aunt and uncle could get to know their future niece-in-law better, when Naylor knew, and she knew, that he was never going to marry her come what may?

Leith had worked herself up into quite a state by the time eleven o'clock ticked round. Naylor didn't even like her, let alone love her, she thought unhappily. And even as her heart leapt when a ring at her doorbell announced that he had arrived, she couldn't hold back a sigh that, when all this was over and he knew how he had been the chief one to be deceived, he would be more likely to throttle her than to merely dismiss her without severance pay.

'I'm ready,' she greeted him coolly as she opened the door, and, not needing to invite him in, dipped back into the hall for her overnight bag.

But Naylor followed her in without invitation and closed the door. 'One thing before we go,' he halted her when with her overnight bag in her hand she turned and looked at him askance. She was still looking at him for enlightenment when he reached into his pocket and drew out a ring which he then proceeded to push at her.

Speechlessly Leith gazed in amazement at the breath-takingly beautiful diamond and emerald engagement ring. Then, as Naylor pushing it at her suddenly came to have some meaning, all hell broke loose within her. 'I'm not wearing *that*!' she told him in no uncertain, heated terms.

Her glance went from the ring to the sudden thrust of his jaw, and she knew she wasn't going to like what was coming—nor did she when he barked, 'Not good enough for you is it?' and that was just about too much.

Suddenly all the emotional stresses and strains she had been under in these past hours all joined up to complete one giant explosion. But, even as she dropped her overnight bag to the floor and her right hand flew through the air, Naylor reacted like lightning, and caught hold of her wrist before her blow could land. But, denied physical release, Leith let fly verbally. 'If you haven't learned by now,' she yelled, 'that I'm not remotely interested in the size of a man's wallet, or what financial gain I can make out of him, or anything else financial apart from the money I make from my own efforts, then *you* need glasses! If you. . .' She hadn't finished, not by a long way, but suddenly she became aware of Naylor shushing her, calming her, gently drawing her into the soothing circle of his arms.

'Shh. . .' he murmured against the side of her head, and for the moment Leith suddenly felt spent, used up, and, for the briefest moment, she gave herself up to the pure heaven of relaxing against him.

Swiftly, though, she gained her second wind, and as wonderful as it felt to have his arms about her, she found some superhuman strength from somewhere to pull back out of his arms.

He let her go, but he was still holding out the ring. 'My aunt, in particular, will look to see if you're wearing an engagement ring,' he murmured coaxingly. And when

Leith stayed stubborn, 'She knows me, Leith, knows that I'd put a ring on my fiancée's finger at the first possible moment.'

Leith looked from the ring to Naylor and, at his waiting look, turned her attention back to the ring. She had a feeling she was being stampeded here, and she didn't very much care for the feeling. She couldn't quite see either, given that Mrs Hepwood obviously knew him as a man who would not drag his feet to give his intended a ring as a token of their promise to marry, that his aunt would be upset in any way if she wasn't wearing a ring. Leith sighed, and knew herself far too weak where Naylor was concerned. And although she felt confused all over again about what this weekend was all about—why she was going, or any of it—she found that, rather than have his aunt ask questions about the absence of a ring, she was stretching out a hand for it.

'Are they real—the stones, I mean?' she asked, her eyes fixed on the large centre emerald and the matching diamond on either side.

'Would I give my love paste?' he mocked, and Leith flicked him a withering look for his trouble, and guessed that, since he wasn't cheap, the ring was the genuine article. She shuddered to think of what it must have cost!

She slipped it over her engagement finger. It fitted perfectly—she had rather thought it would; he was that sort of man. Again, though, just to have Naylor's ring on her finger weakened her and, sorely needing some stiffening, she counteracted that weakness by telling him tartly, 'I'm not used to wearing a ring, so don't blame me if it gets lost!'

'I won't,' he murmured blandly.

'And you're having it back the minute we leave Parkwood!' she told him for good measure.

'Hell's bells,' he mocked, 'we've only been officially

engaged two minutes, and already she's bossing me about!' and, before Leith could find an answer to that, he bent down and picked up her bag, and escorted her out of the apartment block.

The thought of anyone bossing him about and getting away with it amused her, and, strangely, on that journey to Parkwood, she found that she was suddenly starting to feel far more relaxed than she had done.

'Leith, Naylor!' Cicely Hepwood came out to greet them, her husband joining them a minute later as they exchanged greetings on the gravelled drive. 'I've given you the same room as last week,' her hostess bubbled happily as they went into the house. Clearly she was very pleased to see them. 'You'll probably want to go up and wash your hands before lunch, but before you go, I'm just dying to see your engagement ring,' she added excitedly. Then she hesitated, and said more slowly, 'Er—you do have an engagement ring, don't you?'

Leith nodded, but, while giving Naylor top marks for foresight, she couldn't help the wave of emotion that came over her when she brought her left hand up for inspection, 'A very beautiful one too,' she said honestly, and while Mrs Hepwood caught hold of her hand and crooned over the ring, Leith suddenly felt drawn to glance in Naylor's direction. He was watching her, she saw, had his eyes fixed on her and not his aunt or the ring, and, if she wasn't mistaken, he was looking extraordinarily pleased about something.

She pulled her glance away, knowing it couldn't be that he had been pleased that she genuinely thought his choice of ring beautiful. What his pleased look had been about, she realised, was that he'd been proved right, and *had* been right, to buy that ring, in anticipation that it would be the first thing his aunt would look for. At that moment, Leith had a perverse wish to hope she would be around to see his face on the day he realised something he hadn't anticipated—that he'd been had!

With such sweet thoughts she went to her room to restore her equilibrium and to run a comb through her hair before lunch. She was feeling on a much more even keel when, half an hour later, she was seated in the dining-room, in the same place, next to Naylor, that she had sat last weekend.

Conversation throughout the meal was light, cheerful and pleasant, but with no one mentioning the absent member, Travis, until at the end of the meal, just as Guthrie Hepwood had finished asking Naylor's opinion on a wood he was thinking of buying, he added, 'It was Travis's idea originally. He was all into "save the wild-life" at one time, but seems to have had—er—other matters on his mind just lately.'

'I expect it will all come right,' Naylor slotted in soothingly, then, casually, he asked, 'Where is he, by the way?'

It was his aunt who answered, and suddenly Leith knew that behind the smiling front she put up there was a very worried woman when, doing her the compliment of treating Leith like one of the family, Cicely Hepwood replied to her nephew's question, and revealed, 'Travis was definitely wound up about something yesterday, in fact he's been stewing about something all week. Yesterday, though, he seemed worse than ever and. . .' her voice went shaky and she paused a moment before having the self-control to continue '. . .and last night, though he phoned to say not to worry, he didn't come home at all. And,' she ended apprehensively, 'apart from that one time when you went looking for him, he's always been home by this time when he's stayed out before!'

At that point Leith dearly wanted to chip in and say something to relieve the anxiety Mrs Hepwood was going through. But what could she say? It was certain that

Travis hadn't stayed out all night womanising or anything like that. Travis was deeply in love with Rosemary and would never betray his love that way—though she couldn't tell anybody that. Which just left the obvious, that in his unhappiness he had probably gone and got plastered and must, this morning, be taking longer than usual to sleep it off.

Just then, however, Guthrie Hepwood started talking quietly to his wife on the subject of their youngest son, and Leith realised she needn't rack her brains to say anything. He was just talking in terms of betting that Travis would turn up any minute, when Leith, chancing to glance at Naylor, was taken utterly aback. He looked totally infuriated about something, absolutely enraged, and *never* had she seen such hostility in him, such suspicion—and, she realised suddenly, it was all for her!

Feeling badly shaken, Leith switched her glance from him and wondered what in creation she had done now. Then, as a couple of seconds ticked by and her stunned brain began to work, all at once she knew the answer. Suddenly, then, she was hating Naylor Massingham with all that was in her. Because clearly, painfully clearly, the man she had been foolish enough to give her heart to had recalled that, the last time Travis had opted to stay out all night, he had found him in her flat—in bed, so he thought, with her!

Leith hid her hurt, her pain, and began to get mad. So much so that, by the time a general move was made to leave the dining-room, she was feeling boilingly angry with Naylor.

'I think I'll go and get changed,' she remarked to her hostess and, feeling much too heated to want to stay in Naylor's company if they were all adjourning to the drawing-room, she smilingly excused herself and headed for the stairs.

If she was furious, though, so too, she knew, was her

'fiancé', as he too excused himself and went in the same direction. Not trusting herself to say a word to him lest, while his aunt and uncle were within earshot, she spat vitriol at him, Leith chose to ignore him.

That he must be of the same view was obvious when, in grim silence, Naylor kept pace with her over to the staircase and up the stairs.

They were halfway up the stairs when Leith heard the sound of the drawing-room door being closed. Though not one word did either of them utter until they were along the landing outside her bedroom door.

Then, when Leith might well have turned into her room without speaking, he snarled, 'Well?' touching her arm and jerking her round to face him with a none-too-gentle hand.

Leith looked up into his aggressive dark eyes, and wasn't a bit grateful that he'd assumed she had brain enough to work out what this was all about. 'Well what?' she erupted.

'Did you see Travis last night?' he exploded.

'Did he stay the night, you mean! Was he still there when you called for me this morning?' she retorted, and, taking a raw emotional breath, 'Want your ring back?' she felt just enraged enough to taunt—and went to turn her back on him.

She didn't get very far, for something about what she said, or maybe just her insolence in turning away from him, made him more enraged than ever, and, before she could so much as stretch out a hand to the handle of her door, he had caught hold of her and slammed her up against the wall. The next she knew, he was close up against her, and his head was coming down.

'No!' she protested, but it was a protest he had no mind to listen to as his mouth sought and found hers.

Locked in his angry embrace, Leith tried to struggle free, but there was no way Naylor was going to let her free until he was good and ready. His mouth, over hers, was punishing and with nothing in any way gentle about it. Her arms were anchored down by her sides, and at first she tried to use her body to push him away. When he pushed back with his body, she at once realised that all she was succeeding in doing was inciting him to desire.

Knowing how weak he could make her, Leith then grew furious with herself as much as him, and, in that fury, she managed to get her hands on his waist when he had either tired of kissing her or was losing some of his fury. Whatever it was, on pushing at him with every scrap of her strength, she suddenly found herself free and wasn't waiting around for answers. In a flash she had her bedroom door open. She vaguely thought she heard him groan, 'Oh hell!' but she wasn't waiting around to check that out either as she rapidly put herself one side of her bedroom door, and left Naylor at the other.

Leaning her weight against the door, she half feared he would force his way in. But, after about a minute of holding her breath and with not so much as a scratch sounding on the woodwork, she realised that he must have gone away.

She drew a shaky breath and, feeling more confused than ever, went to sit in a bedroom chair. Ten minutes later she was more collected as she changed into trousers and a shirt while at the same time she wondered what she was doing. Surely what she should be doing was packing her bag and getting out of there.

How could she leave, though? Both Mr and Mrs Hepwood would think it most odd. And, since they regarded Naylor like a son, they had enough to worry about over Travis without having the added worry of Naylor's love-life looking as though it had hit stormy waters.

Leith wandered over to the window and stared out at the sun-filled afternoon, suddenly too restless to want to stay in her room until it was time for dinner. She decided to go for a long walk—with luck she needn't see Naylor before dinner.

Questions about his actions, his brutal kiss, were chasing about in her head as she made her way down the stairs. But she had an idea that she wouldn't at all like the answers if she started to probe into why he had been so furious or why he had been so goaded as to manhandle her and brutally kiss her the way he had. Somehow, she felt sure it would all end up being her fault anyway!

The drawing-room door was closed, she observed as she reached the hall, and she was very much tempted to go straight out of the front door without a word to anyone. But, even though she had no idea what she would say should her hosts ask where Naylor was, she realised that, as a guest, she owed Mr and Mrs Hepwood the courtesy of telling them where she was going.

She crossed the hall to the drawing-room door, pinned a pleasant smile on her face, and went in. Then she discovered that she need not have worried that her hosts might ask where Naylor was, because Mr and Mrs Hepwood were not in the drawing-room. In fact, the only person who was in the drawing-room was Naylor himself.

She stopped dead in her tracks and was about to turn hastily round when he called her name and, oddly, seemed to her to be as restless as she. She saw his glance go down to her left hand, and quickly hurried into speech herself.

'I was looking for Mrs Hepwood,' she said quickly, then discovered that she was staring at his mouth, the mouth that had so brutally kissed hers and, illogically, she suddenly felt an urge to go to him and kiss him, as though with a gentle kiss to wipe out what had been.

She blinked, and knew he'd think her mad if she did anything of the sort—or, worse, think her in love with him.

'What do you want my aunt for?' he asked, and was suspicious again, she saw.

'Not to tell her anything I shouldn't!' Leith snapped tartly, her softer tendencies swiftly buried. 'I merely thought I should let her know I'm going out for a long walk.'

'My aunt's upstairs,' he told her, and she turned to go. But he urgently called her name again and, reluctantly, she turned back. 'Leith, I——' he began more slowly, but someone coming in through the open french doors caused him to break off.

'Travis!' Leith exclaimed as she recognised his cousin. But, even while she was thinking that Mrs Hepwood would be much relieved to see her son, Leith's eyes were opening wide. For Travis was not alone; he had brought someone with him. 'Rosemary!' she gasped in absolute astonishment, and went forward to give her friend a warm hug.

'I thought Mother and Dad might be in here, so we took a short cut across the lawn,' Travis, a cock-a-hoop Travis, explained, a Travis who was looking the happiest Leith had ever seen him. 'I'm glad you're here, Leith,' he went on, 'you deserve to be the first to know——'

'You phoned Rosemary——' she began to guess.

'I did better than that,' he replied, placing a possessive arm about Rosemary's shoulders. 'After spending a foul night thinking I'd go mad if I didn't get something sorted soon, I went down to Dorset this morning and——'

'You went to Hazelbury? To Rosemary's home?' Leith questioned in amazement.

'I couldn't take it any more,' he answered. 'It seemed to me that the longer Rosemary stayed with her parents, the longer they'd have to put the pressure on in enforcing their beliefs on her. Anyhow, I was shaking like a leaf when I told Mr and Mrs Green I wanted to marry their daughter, and——'

'*Marry*!' The exclamation had come from Naylor. All eyes turned to him. Oh, help, Leith thought, recognising from Naylor's expression that somebody's head was going to roll when he realised what had been going on—and she had a dreadful feeling it was going to be hers.

'Too true!' Travis replied to Naylor enthusiastically, clearly on cloud nine and in no state to notice what threatening expression anyone might wear. 'It's also true, isn't it, darling,' he said to Rosemary, giving her a squeeze, 'that you were coming to the end of your tether too in Hazelbury? Anyhow,' he went on to tell Naylor and Leith, 'Rosemary was magnificent, and when I asked her parents what they loved most, respectability or their daughter, and they showed me the door, Rosemary told them she'd decided to give Derek the divorce he wanted, and that she was coming with me.'

'Would someone mind telling me,' Naylor cut in quietly—too quietly, Leith thought, 'what the *hell* is going on?'

For a moment Travis looked taken off his stride at his cousin's question. But in a moment he was all smiles again. 'Sorry, Naylor,' he apologised. 'I'm so over the moon, I'm forgetting you don't know Rosemary. Though I'm sure Leith, despite my begging her to keep my confidences, will have told you how Rosemary hails from the same village in Dorset, but normally has a flat across the hall from Leith in London.'

Leith felt she really should say something, but what? Then, 'Go on,' Naylor was urging, his voice to her ears sounding more ominously quiet than ever.

'Leith, though she'll have been far too modest to tell you,' Travis obliged cheerfully, 'was an enormous help to Rosemary and me when we first met. Then when, because Rosemary was having a few problems, she refused to see me, Leith, as well as acting as go-between for us, also put up with my heartache and—I own—drunkenness on one night in particular, when because I was too sloshed to drive, she deposited me on Sebastian's bed and left me to sleep it off.'

Leith dared a look at Naylor—oh, grief! she thought as she recognised that he was simmering, none too gently. 'So——!' he began to demand, but just then both Travis's mother and father entered the drawing-room, and, in the ensuing happy chaos, he chose to swallow what he had been going to say.

'Travis!' Cicely cried joyously, and, her glance going to the pretty young woman whom he still had an arm around, 'You've brought a friend to see us,' she beamed.

'Rosemary's more than a friend,' Travis answered proudly. 'Mother, come and meet the woman I'm going to marry.'

'*Travis!*'

Suddenly everyone seemed to be talking at once. Leith took a look at the still open french doors. Now seemed as good a time as any to go for the walk she had promised herself. A quick glance at Naylor showed that he was, for the moment, taken up with watching not only Travis and Rosemary, but his aunt and uncle and their reaction to the bombshell that their youngest had just dropped.

In a trice Leith slipped quickly and silently through the french doors. Once on the lawns, though, she looked at the route she would take, and suddenly felt vulnerable. It was open countryside that way—somehow she didn't want to be seen.

Not far away to the left stood the summerhouse. It faced the open countryside, the view. Hoping it was open, Leith went fleetfootedly over to it.

Luck was with her as the glass-fronted door yielded to her touch. She went in, saw that it was larger than it looked from outside, and that it housed some very comfortable wooden-framed, plump-cushioned furniture.

With her head buzzing with all that had just taken place, she sank down on a padded sofa, and was overwhelmingly glad that at last it looked as though Travis and Rosemary might have some joy from the love they shared.

She felt admiration for Travis and the fact that, plainly worn down by his unending unhappiness, he had taken the bull by the horns and had gone to see Rosemary and her parents. Leith realised she would no doubt get to hear more about it later, but she felt admiration for Rosemary too in that, while she would take no end of an emotional battering on her own behalf, the fact of her parents turning on the man she loved had brought out her fighting, protective instincts.

With thoughts of Naylor pushing and pushing to get through, though, it wasn't long before both Travis and Rosemary went from Leith's mind as she found she could no longer hold back from again seeing Naylor's simmering expression. There had been something menacing in that look too, she thought. But, as she acknowledged that Naylor had always been swift with his summing up, she somehow had the shaky feeling that the hour of retribution was near.

At that precise moment she heard a footstep. Her head jerked up as a shadow came to the glass-fronted door of the summerhouse, and Leith swallowed hard. For she knew then, as she recognised the tall man with his hand on the door-handle, that retribution was nearer than that—seconds away, in fact. Clearly Naylor had decided to try the summerhouse before the stables and beyond. Clearly he had come looking for her!

She had her eyes glued on him when, his expression

unrelenting, he entered the summerhouse. Her eyes stayed on him as in a deliberate kind of movement he closed the door with a chilling click.

Then he stood, and for long moments he just looked down at her, scrutinising her from his lofty height. Then, 'So,' he clipped, in tough, hard tones, 'start talking.'

Woodenly Leith stared at him. She had known from the beginning that he would be furiously angry when he knew how he'd been led up the garden path, and she tried hard to keep her cool. But she knew, as, silent, watching and hostile, he waited, that things had never looked more favourable for a blazing row!

CHAPTER NINE

FEELING a desperate need to swallow hard again, Leith held down the urge. That Naylor was incensed was obvious. But, since he'd said not another word after that 'So, start talking' she thought it might be an idea if she made some sort of reply quickly.

'What—about?' she asked, and saw at once, when he took a long temper-controlling breath, that her reply had not gone down very well.

'I warn you now,' he clipped, 'I'm in no mood for games.' He jerked his head in the direction of the house. 'You can begin by telling me what the devil all *that* was about!'

Leith had never felt so churned up inside, but she made valiant attempts to stay in one piece, and, to her own surprise, effected an offhand shrug. 'I thought it was all fairly self-explanatory,' she replied coolly.

She saw his eyes narrow, and, as his hands clenched down by his sides, she recalled thinking once not so long ago that he'd probably throttle her when he learned of the way she'd deceived him. He did not throttle her, however, but, clearly better able to see her face and her expression from that spot, and obviously thinking that to get her to reveal everything looked like being a long job, he hooked one of the wooden-framed chairs to him, and sat down opposite her.

Then, while she was inwardly quaking and realising, since he was now effectively blocking the door, that, if she had wanted to shorten this interview she should have immediately started to gabble out every word that he wanted to know, he leaned forward and, his chin jutting aggressively, grated, 'So, we'll start again. Now,' he said heavily, 'who the hell is Sebastian?'

Feeling quite astonished that his first question was not about Travis, or any one of the many questions he might have asked on the subject of the way she'd led him on a false trail, she began, 'He's—er—in—er—India, at the——'

'My st. . .' Naylor bit back some explosive utterance. Then, plainly a man now very much aware of having been duped, and who was not going to stand for a second helping—therefore now hell bent on having every I dotted, every T crossed—in actuality, on leaving nothing to be guessed at, 'Your brother, in fact! Your only brother?'

'Sebastian's my only brother,' Leith could see no harm in admitting—then found that his questions about her brother didn't end there.

'How long has he been in India?' he shot at her, and Leith blamed her present confusion that, when he seemed to want the answer quickly, she couldn't for the moment remember.

'Not long,' she replied.

'This year? Only months, in fact?' he questioned, and, when she nodded, 'Before he went to India, the two of you shared your flat?'

'True,' she answered snappily, starting to grow a little irritated at his bludgeoning questioning. Then she saw a sudden sharp look come into Naylor's eyes and knew something had just made sense to him.

'You shared your mortgage with him too, didn't you?' he didn't hesitate to delve into her finances.

'If you must know,' Leith erupted, 'we were buying the flat jointly, and, to save your asking,' she inserted acidly, since it seemed he wanted the lot, 'we put down a deposit from some money left to us by our grandfather.'

She'd made a mistake, it seemed, for Naylor appeared

not the least interested in the sum they had put down,
or her grandfather, though he was still homed on to the
Sebastian theme when he charged, 'But your brother left
and stuck you with the mortgage by not making provi-
sion to pay his half in his absence?'

'He forgot, I exp——' Leith began to defend
Sebastian, then stopped short. 'It's got nothing to do
with you!' she fired rudely, and—oh, grief! she thought
as Naylor's expression went grim. She knew she was in
trouble before he spoke.

'It's got everything to do with me, *woman*!' he roared
grimly. 'You played me for a jackass, and *nobody* does
that, not even you, without good reason!'

She had no idea what that 'not even you' meant, but
she wasn't in the business of waiting to find out. 'I had
good reason!' she cried angrily, her voice rising.

'How?'

'You asked for it!'

'Again—how?'

'My sainted aunt, you've got a bad memory! From the
first, from the moment we met that night you came
looking for Travis, you've——'

'We'll get to Travis in a minute,' he chopped her off—
and, ever a man who was not going to be deterred from
his initial line of questioning, 'Before that, you can tell
me why, when *deigning* to let me know you had a brother,
you deliberately withheld the fact that his name was
Sebastian—a fact which would have straight away
cleared up the fact of there being more than one man in
your life when I came along!'

To hear him tell it, you'd think he really and truly was
her fiancé! she thought. 'With your opinion of me at
ground level, I should want to do anything to improve
it!' she exploded furiously, ousting any weakening
thoughts imagining being his fiancée for real brought.

'Which is why, of course, you never once mentioned

that until recently your brother lived with you and paid half the mortgage, thereby making your flat affordable. Which is also why you deliberately allowed me to think that your flat has only one bedroom when clearly there are two. Which is——'

'As I recall it,' Leith cut him off sharply, 'you were in no mood that night you came looking for Travis to want a conducted tour around the estate!'

'You could have set me straight!'

'Like blazes I could! You'd made up your mind about me before you'd even met me!'

'Some woman was making Travis unhappy—he was at your flat—in my book, it had to be you!'

'Well, you've just found out it wasn't me, but my friend and neighbour, and——'

'And you've been looking forward to this day, haven't you?' Naylor cut in harshly.

'Looking forward?'

'Hell fire!' he exploded, 'I'll bet there were times when you found it hard not to laugh in my face!'

'I'm only human!' Leith declared, taking jolly good care he should never know of the times she'd been nearer to tears than laughter on his account.

Then she discovered that he hadn't finished yet, when, fiercely, he began to probe the core of it all, 'Why did you allow me to think you were my cousin's mistress?' he demanded, 'When——'

'From what I remember of it,' she cut in hostilely, 'you wouldn't have believed me had I told you anything else! You were determined to think me some—some harpy, with my eyes only on Travis's wallet!'

'You didn't even *try* to tell me differently!' he accused harshly. 'He was in bed in your flat, but you said nothing about how he'd formed a serious attachment for your married neighbour, who, according to Travis, is having a few problems!'

'Apart from the fact that Rosemary was anxious that no one knew of her friendship with Travis,' Leith found she was having to defend, 'so far as I knew, I wasn't ever going to see you again.'

'Hmph,' he grunted, and suddenly paused. Then as he rubbed a thoughtful hand over his chin, it seemed as though she had reminded him of something—and all at once he was easing off the pressure, to remark reminiscently, 'It was a—surprise to me too, to glance through your office in passing the following Monday, and see your chestnut head.'

'You recognised me?'

'You had your back to me, and the screwed-back hair style was unfamiliar. But,' his eyes went to her long shining tresses, 'that glorious colour drew me.'

Leith swallowed, and wasn't certain that she didn't want him back to being blunt, fierce and aggressive. With his tone softening—without his complimentary remark about her hair—she was finding it extremely difficult to cope. 'I—er—didn't know you were—um—Naylor Massingham—my boss,' she explained.

'And I didn't know that the woman they called Miss Frostbite was the chestnut-haired beauty I'd tangled with early on Sunday morning,' he replied.

Oh, Naylor, don't! Leith thought jumpily, and the fact that he, the most important person in her world, thought her beautiful, caused her to have to fight harder than ever to find some sharp reply. 'Yes, well,' she said lamely, but found some help as she recalled his arrogant, sarcastic manner that day. 'Well, it didn't take you long once you did know to give me an ultimatum about my job if I didn't give Travis up!'

'A fat lot of good that did!' he rapped, his softer tone soon gone. Perversely, Leith wanted the less aggressive Naylor back. 'That very evening, while I was out to dinner with a friend, who should I see in that self-same restaurant but my cousin with a possessive hand on the arm of none other than you?'

'Possessive!' Leith retorted, quite well able to do without Naylor referring to *his* dinner companion, his beautiful *blonde* dinner companion, and *friend*. 'Travis was merely guiding me over to your table, as I recall it.'

'Why then, if you weren't his girlfriend, did you agree to dine with him?' Naylor demanded aggressively.

'If you must know,' she snapped, 'because Rosemary had gone to stay with her parents the Friday before and wasn't back, and, because of their—her parents', I mean—unyielding attitude on the issue of divorce, Rosemary didn't dare tell them she'd got a boyfriend—much less would she allow Travis to contact her there.'

'Huh!' Naylor snorted sourly, and still pressed, 'None of which explains what *you* were doing dining with him,' and, while it didn't surprise Leith that he had got her so mixed up that she hadn't answered him properly, what did surprise her was that Naylor should suddenly come across as sounding jealous!

A moment later she brushed any such crazy notion aside. If there was any jealousy floating around, it was all on her side over his blonde friend. 'I went out to dinner with Travis because, apart from Rosemary asking me to look after him, I'd never seen or heard him so unhappy,' she explained flatly. 'I'm fond of him,' she further stated, saw from Naylor's frown that he didn't go overboard about her affection for his cousin, but went determinedly on, 'I'm fond of them both, but when Travis rang, sounding so despairing, I accepted his dinner invitation, knowing that he needed to talk about Rosemary. It never occurred to me,' she ended shortly, if honestly, 'that you'd be dining at the same place.'

'I'll bet it didn't!' Naylor hammered at her. 'So why, the next time I saw you, couldn't you explain any of this?'

Leith had an excellent memory of the next time she'd seen him. He'd come to her flat, and he'd kissed her, and she'd gone to bed unable to forget his kiss—and her response to it. 'I couldn't tell you, or explain,' she tried to push away such memories, 'because by then Travis had expressly asked me not to mention a word to a soul about Rosemary.' Suddenly, she was overcome by a feeling of remorse. 'I'm sorry if that hurts—you being family and everything,' she murmured sensitively, 'but things were really desperate for him with Rosemary. I—just couldn't—break my word to him.'

'Obviously!' Naylor rapped bluntly. 'You were——' Abruptly he broke off. Unexpectedly, as though something important had just struck him, he was still—and Leith was wary. Without knowing what was going through his head, she remembered his lightning brain, the way, in less than a second, he'd worked out that she had left Ardis & Co through no fault of her own. 'You couldn't break your word to Travis,' he resumed slowly, a sharp, alert look about him as he watched her, 'because you were fond of him, right?'

'Er—yes, I suppose so,' she conceded, not given to breaking her word anyhow, but wondering anxiously what it was his brain was sifting through now. There was something in his look, that way he was watching her as though not intending to miss a thing, which she found a little worrying.

'So does it follow,' he began to ask carefully, deliberately, 'that you likewise couldn't break your word to me—for the same reason?' Her eyes shot wide in alarm, and that was before—making her panic wildly—he followed on in a taut kind of voice, 'Can I take it, Leith, that you are—in some degree—fond of me?'

She had no idea how he could have drawn such a conclusion, and rushed to deny it. 'Wh. . . Don't. . . Of course not!' she fell over her words in her rush—and found that such a denial did her not a scrap of good.

'Why, then,' he went on doggedly, 'when I specifically told you not to tell Travis that our 'mutual attraction' was a put-up affair, did you—by staying silent—keep your word to me?'

'I. . . How. . .' Desperately Leith tried to pull herself together. Then to her utmost relief she found she had a stray particle of grey matter still working. 'You know why,' she collected herself to articulate. 'My job was on the line if I told him any——'

'But,' he stopped her, 'you gave in your notice last Tuesday.'

'I know, but. . .' She was floundering, and, having so to speak just shot herself in the foot, was forced to make it up as she went along. 'I haven't seen Travis to tell him anything,' she declared hurriedly—and was made to sit there while Naylor looked at her long and steadily.

Her heart was racing in panic when he said, 'Clearly you hadn't decided to resign your job on Monday, or you would have told Travis when he came to the office to have a quick word with you then.' Confound her brain, Leith thought, she'd forgotten about having seen Travis on Monday. 'But,' Naylor was going on, 'perhaps you thought to tell him that you weren't truly engaged to me, and all about it, when you saw him this weekend?'

Leith was lost, though she was still doing her very best. 'I—er—don't know what you're getting at,' she muttered bravely—and nearly went into heart failure at his reply.

For he paused, and, though she was positive it was a trick of the light, she could have sworn he looked slightly unsure of himself. 'I confess, my dear, to be in such a turmoil of desperation that I hardly know anything myself any more,' he drawled. And, while Leith was striving to recover from the fact of his calling her 'my dear', he was adding firmly, 'Except that, regarding Travis as a much-loved brother as I do, there was no way I would have let him take you away from me.'

Her throat went dry, and she moved a fraction from her seat. Then she saw that since Naylor was still blocking the doorway, she couldn't get up and run, unless he moved first. She met his steady look head-on, and realised that he had no intention of moving until all that was making him desperate had been said.

'I. . .' she tried to get release from her choky throat, and coughed, then succeeded. 'T-take me from T-Travis? I—don't think I—er—understand.'

'You're sharp, you're intelligent, Leith, I think you understand very well,' he countered, but with her heart drumming away inside her body Leith was totally unable to believe what it seemed Naylor was hinting at, and could only stare wordlessly. Naylor waited several long seconds, then when it seemed she was going to say nothing and that it was all up to him, he pulled his chair up closer to hers and then, drawing a long steadying breath, told her, 'After the hard time I've given you, I suppose it's no more than I deserve that I should—um—give a little, before I can hope to take what's mine.'

Her wide green eyes stayed fixed on him. 'You're. . .' she began, but had to pause and take a shaky breath before she could go on. 'You're talking—in riddles,' she uttered in a voice that was barely audible.

'Which doesn't surprise me,' he agreed, and, to cause her yet more disquiet, 'I've been on one hell of a merry-go-round since soon after I met you.'

Her wide eyes went saucer-wide. 'You're—serious?' she choked, with no intention of running from him now—indeed, she felt glued to her seat.

'I've never been more serious,' he replied solemnly. Then he said clearly, his eyes ever watchful on her face,

'Without my acknowledging it, I've been seriously attracted to you from the start.'

Leith had to swallow before she could speak. If this—what Naylor was saying about being attracted to her—was all part and parcel of his retribution for what she'd done, then she'd somehow take it. But she felt starved for a word, a crumb, of some regard from him, and just could not find the words to tell him that she didn't want to hear. She *did* want to hear, and, whether she ended up very bruised and very wounded or no, she was ready to give him any encouragement she could.

You—have?' she questioned, her backbone feeling like so much jelly. 'Fr-from that first night in my flat?'

'Oh, yes,' he told her gently. 'I wasn't acknowledging it then, of course. I was too busy then damning the sort of woman I thought you were, who could take my happy-go-lucky cousin and turn him into the tormented, drunken wreck I half carried out of your flat that night.'

'He's—had a tough time of it,' Leith sympathised, then found that, if she had any sympathy for anyone, Naylor didn't want her to have it for anyone but him.

'So have I!' he stated abruptly, but went on more evenly, 'You weren't out of my head yet when not much more than a day later I was walking back to my office from the contracts department, and saw another chestnut head. I had a meeting to chair, so I didn't have time to stop and make the acquaintance of the one member of staff I'd missed. But what did I find I was doing but forgetting my meeting and going in to say "Hello" to Miss Leithia Everett.'

'On—er—on account of my. . .the colour of my hair?'

'Believe it,' he replied, and continued. 'And then, having been shaken when you turned and I discovered that only one woman has hair that glorious colour, I went on to my meeting, finding it incredible that, instead of dismissing you from my employment on the spot, I'd actually done nothing of the kind.'

'You felt—you should have dismissed me?' Leith asked quickly.

'It should have been instinctive in me to do so—yet it wasn't,' he owned. 'What I did do was to warn you not to see my cousin again. But only,' he added with a self-derisory look, 'to find out just how much notice you took of that when that same evening you went out to dinner with him.'

'You were—angry?'

'I was furious,' he admitted, and added, 'and something else, as well.'

'Oh?' she questioned, hardly daring to believe that this serious though pleasant man was the same man who she'd thought would come gunning for her with a vengeance when he discovered that she was not, and never had been, Travis's girlfriend.

'If you're asking what that something else was, then. . .' He broke off as though *he* needed a moment of strength, then he revealed '. . .then it could only be—jealousy.'

'*Jealousy!*' Leith exclaimed, her lips parting in her disbelief.

'What else?' he confirmed quietly. 'It was the same feeling that raged in me the next evening when I came to your home and suspected for some seconds that you had a male guest waiting for you in your bedroom.'

'Good—heavens!' she gasped faintly, but it was not an exclamation over his suspicions, but because it was starting to dawn on her that he really *had* been jealous. 'Y-you kissed me!' she recalled, in quick agitation needing to say something as hope suddenly began to spiral upward, the fact that Naylor had kissed her being her most vivid memory of that night.

'I haven't forgotten,' he answered softly, his eyes

searching her face, though what he was looking for Leith
had no clue. 'I'd meant it to be a cold, calculating test.
I'd meant to kiss you, while keeping detached. Then
suddenly you were starting to yield and I was having to
fight like the very devil to remember if there had ever
been a reason for your being in my arms—other than the
obvious one, that you were beautiful and that I was
enjoying the experience.'

'I—er—hmm. . .couldn't believe I'd—responded the
way I did, afterwards,' Leith found she was confessing.

Naylor stretched out a hand and took hold of one of
hers in her lap. Then, pausing, he asked quietly, 'Does
that mean anything, Leith?'

'I—er. . .' She was having an awful job not to swallow
again. 'It—m-might,' she admitted nervously.

'Such as. . .' he began to urge, then broke off, and,
his other hand suddenly coming to take hold of her left
one, he leaned forward and with both his hands holding
hers, looked deeply, intently, into her eyes, 'You're not
sure of what it is I've been saying, are you?' he asked,
and when Leith just stared dumbly back at him, 'I
haven't said enough, have I?' he queried.

'You. . .' Leith found her voice. 'You—this—you're
not—it isn't part of my punishment for what I did—for
the way I didn't tell you about Rosemary and. . .'

'*Punishment!*' he exclaimed, appalled. 'Oh, my little
love, *no*! From what I've been able to gather, you've
been utterly fantastic in helping Travis keep his
sanity. . .' He broke off, and, while Leith's heart was
violently thudding because Naylor—barely realising it,
she thought, but as though it was the way he thought of
her—had called her his little love, he had latched on to
that word 'punishment' and, his fingers crushing hers,
demanded, 'Would it truly be a punishment to you if
everything I've so far said was not the truth?'

'I never have enjoyed being lied to,' she replied after

some moments of inner struggle—and had to give Naylor top marks for the fact that, when he could well have accused *her* of lying by omission, he did not, for she had deliberately omitted to tell him that she and Travis were no more than friends.

What he did say, however, was enough to have her gripping hard on to his hands, and staring at him in wonderment. 'I'm not lying to you, Leith. I've known the rage of jealousy over you, and have known for some time now that the reason why I don't want any other man to touch you is that I want you myself.'

'You w-want me?' she questioned on a wobbly note. But, when she would have preferred her voice to come out without that tremor to it, Naylor, she discovered, seemed to have taken heart from her shaky tone. She realised too, as, large-eyed, loving and anxious, she stared at him as he again searched her face, that this time he must have found what he was looking for. Because suddenly he let go his hold on her hands and tenderly cupped her face.

'Leith, my sweet one,' he whispered, 'I—*love* and want you.'

'You l-love me?' she gasped, wanting with all she had to believe it, but somehow finding it too inconceivable to be true.

'With my whole heart,' he told her sincerely, and, seeming to read her inner tumult, 'Have you any objection if I join you on that sofa?' he asked—but he appeared to be asking more than that.

It was then Leith saw that if she told him she had no objection, she would not only be inviting him to sit beside her, but inviting him also to tell her anything that he wanted to.

Wordlessly, encouragingly, she moved up to make room for him. She saw his brow clear, and became aware that he had been under every bit as much strain as herself. Swiftly he moved and, seated beside her, turned to look at her and to take hold of her hands again.

Though he seemed all at once nervously on edge, as he asked, 'Can you not tell me, dear Leith, how you feel to know that I love you with all my heart?'

She did have to swallow then, but her voice was husky and emotional as she replied, 'I—can't believe it.'

Solemnly Naylor looked down into her face. 'Do you *want* to believe it?' he asked tensely. Leith stared silently back at him, and, when her voice defeated her, there was only one thing she could do. She nodded, and suddenly saw all the tension leave him. 'Then I'll make you believe it,' he breathed softly, and gently, tenderly, he enfolded her in his arms.

Leith felt near to tears at the beauty of it, at the wonder of it, when unhurriedly Naylor held her close up against his heart, and, reverently almost, placed his warm, giving mouth over hers.

'Oh, Naylor!' she cried as he broke his kiss, and knew yet more heaven when, after long seconds of looking down, his eyes devouring her face, he placed whispers of kisses on her eyes and forehead.

'Do you love me, my darling?' he asked, holding her in the close confines of one arm and brushing her hair back from her face with a caressing hand. 'I want to believe it too, but while your eyes show you have some feeling for me, I need, I'm afraid, to hear it.'

He smiled encouragingly. Leith smiled back, then, shyly, 'I love you so much, Naylor,' she murmured huskily.

'My darling!' he cried exultantly, and just had to kiss her again.

All was silent in the summerhouse for long minutes as, in the mutual heart's-ease of each other's arms, they clung to each other and kissed, and kissed and held, and kissed again to pull back and to stare at each other, all barriers down. Then they held each other close again, and gradually disbelief changed to belief. And, locked in a warm embrace, they both realised that what had once seemed unattainable now started to become reality.

'My sweet, sweet, adorable Leith,' murmured Naylor, and, tucking her head comfortably into his shoulder, 'I know I've not done the least thing to earn it—but tell me again.'

'That—I love you?'

'And again.'

'I love you,' Leith laughed.

'You incredible woman! I'm hopelessly all yours,' he told her warmly.

'How come I never guessed?' she teased, shy still, although the barriers had gone.

'You weren't supposed to guess,' he growled mock-fiercely. '*I* was having enough problems with trying to understand what was happening to me without wanting you—the cause of many a sleepless night, I might mention—knowing of my weakness.'

Leith could never see Naylor being weak, but she queried, 'You've had sleepless nights too?'

'You as well?' he asked incredulously, and grinned quite cheerfully when she nodded.

'You were saying you couldn't understand?' Leith took up, wanting to know everything there was to know about him, yet not knowing quite where to start.

'Neither could I understand,' he answered. 'Not until I realised why my head was so constantly full of you could I understand, first of all, why it was that I wouldn't dismiss you. It was only later that I realised it wasn't that I wouldn't, but that I couldn't dismiss you—and I knew it was because I wanted you Monday to Friday where I could see you if I wanted to.'

'Really?' Leith gasped—then had to smile. 'You

rogue—you threatened to dismiss me—and without pay!'

'I was in panic.'

'Panic? You?'

'I just couldn't face a weekend of not seeing you, but, when you refused to come with me this weekend and seemed about to march out of my office, I panicked and had threatened to dismiss you before I knew what I was doing.'

'Oh, Naylor!' Leith crooned softly.

'My darling,' he murmured, and, clearly enchanted at her tone, her crooning his name, he kissed her, then pulled back to tell her throatily, 'You've triggered all manner of emotions in me, my love—some I never so much as suspected I was capable of.'

'Honestly?' she asked, while growing more and more confident of his love all the time, although it still felt too utterly, wonderfully fantastic to be real.

'Oh, sweet Leith,' he breathed, 'if only you knew! The jealousy, the despair, the fury, the hope, the black depths. . .' He broke off. 'Believe me, you'd never doubt what's in my heart for you.'

Leith looked at him with gentle green eyes, her heart drumming tenderly for him. 'You've been jealous——' she began.

'I've been drowning in it,' he broke in. 'If it wasn't some man named Sebastian——'

'What did you do with his hat?' Leith remembered.

'I'll get him another,' Naylor replied, with a grin, totally unashamed, and went on, 'If it wasn't him getting to me, then I was being turned inside out with jealousy over Travis. And that before I touched on any of the other men in your life.'

'Other men? There aren't any,' Leith laughed.

'I wasn't to know that!' he growled, looking delighted by her laughter. 'I was eaten alive by jealousy when I happened across you in the arms of that Fisher chap from your department that day.'

'You were jealous of Paul F. . .' Her voice faded out, and Naylor nodded.

'Even though I quickly realised that you objected strongly to him having his arms around you, that didn't stop my initial uproar of jealousy.'

'You reported him to Robert Drewer,' Leith recalled.

'Too true! I'm not having that sort of harassment going on in my business, and most definitely not when it concerns you.' Naylor suddenly gave a lop-sided grin as he went on, 'And if you think I've got a nerve after the way I've harassed you then, in my defence, you, my love, were giving me a load of grief which I was having an enormous amount of trouble handling.'

'Me?' she exclaimed innocently.

'Who else did I think constantly about over the weekend following the Fisher incident?'

'Me?' she queried rapturously.

'Who else?' He laughed, and she simply adored the way his face lit up when he laughed. 'Is it any wonder that I could barely wait for you to get into your office on Monday before I rang you to come and see me?'

Leith just beamed at him. 'I thought you wanted to see me about the Palmer & Pearson file, but you told me you'd decided to take me over as your girlfriend.'

'And I can't now be anything but glad that you kept quiet about never having been my cousin's girlfriend in the first place.'

'I thought you'd commit murder when you knew what I'd done—er—hadn't done.'

'I might have, were I not so entirely in love with you,' he smiled. But he was serious as he added, 'I then decided, since you were so career-minded to want my word that your job would still be yours, that you should have plenty to do.'

'You instructed my head of department to see to it that I had to take work home in order to keep on top?' she questioned, without heat.

'Forgive me, but I hadn't sorted out yet who Sebastian was, and while I was too stubbornly proud to ask, I was tormented enough by jealousy to want you to have little time or energy for socialising. Jealousy,' he confessed, 'has been like a curse on me. If it wasn't Travis, then it was Sebastian, and, that evening when I sat for a whole hour outside your apartment block waiting for you—when I've never waited an hour for any woman in my life!—I was bombarded by images of your being out with yet some other man.'

'I'd gone flat-hunting.'

'So you later told me, but at that time, while I was growing more and more tormented by the second, some mulishness in me insisted that I should hang on a few more minutes, and then another few more minutes. I took some work out of my briefcase, but, as I waited to see who you came home with, my concentration,' he owned, 'was not what it should have been.'

'I came home alone,' Leith murmured softly.

'And when I was furious, you laughed at me—and I knew then that I loved you with my whole being.'

'You knew then?'

'I knew it, with certainty,' he replied tenderly. 'Yet before I could spend an hour just delighting in your sole company, along came Travis, and I was so crucified by the thought that he'd been your lover, I had to leave for fear I might give myself away.'

Leith stared at him with gentle adoring eyes. 'If it's any help,' she began quietly, 'I seem to have formed an aversion to you speaking to blondes—particularly blondes by the name of Olinda.'

'Truly?' he exclaimed, and looked quite delighted at the thought. He kissed her warmly anyhow, then, while her heart was still beating erratically from his kiss, it seemed he just had to ask, 'Do you know when it was that you first felt something for me—other than hate?'

'If you're asking when did I know I was in love with you,' Leith replied huskily, 'I can tell you exactly. It was last Saturday. We'd—you and I—we'd gone for a walk and you'd made some remark——'

'Some offensive, jealous and quite uncalled-for remark,' he recalled.

Leith smiled, entirely unoffended. 'And I hit you, and——'

'And I deserved it, every power-packed ounce of it.'

'You defeat me when you agree with me,' she laughed.

'I'll remember that,' he grinned—but he had not lost sight of what he wanted to know. 'Carry on,' he ordered.

'That's it,' she smiled. 'I raced back to the house, furious, hurt and upset—and just knew I wouldn't feel anywhere near as hurt were it not for the fact that I loved you.'

At once Naylor gathered her closer, and tenderly kissed her as though to kiss away any trace of hurt he had ever inflicted. 'Will it help you to forgive me, sweetheart, if I tell you that I spent most of that Saturday in torment?'

'I'll forgive you anything,' she offered freely, but just had to ask, 'You weren't happy to be back in your old home?'

'It wasn't that so much but the realisation that I hated it every time over lunch when you looked across at Travis and smiled. When I followed you back from our walk and found you in the library with him—and holding fondly on to his arm—I was convinced you were still playing around with him.'

'Oh, Naylor,' Leith mourned, 'I only went to the library with Travis because he wanted to phone Rosemary, and he asked me to make the call in case her

parents were home. Which they were,' she went on
when, incredibly to her, Naylor seemed to need to hear
more. 'Travis did speak to Rosemary, but because her
parents were there it was a nothing sort of conversation—
and he was very upset afterwards.'

'So,' Naylor commented, with a lop-sided grin she
was beginning to love, 'was I.'

'Is that why you announced at dinner that night that
you and I were engaged?'

'It seemed, since it was plain to me by then that you'd
no intention of finishing with Travis, that by announcing
our engagement I'd have done it for you. For my sins,'
he went on, 'you, in your fury at what I'd done, made
me furious by pretending to be all loving. I wanted you
loving, without the acting,' he confessed.

'I'm sorry,' she murmured softly.

'It's I who should apologise,' he declared quickly,
following on, 'A devil of some sort came over me when,
at your bedroom door that night, you goaded me to
jealousy beyond enduring by daring to remind me that
there were some nights when you couldn't bear to let
Travis go home.' He drew a long breath as though even
now the memory still haunted him. 'I terrified you,
didn't I?'

'Er—not so much,' she replied, and remembering
how loving him, his kisses, his ardour, had driven her
wild with desire, 'only—only at the beginning,' she
owned, but suddenly halted when his expression altered
and all at once he looked totally winded. 'What is it?'
she asked urgently. 'What have I——?'

'You. . . That night,' he uttered shakenly, 'you said
then that you were a virgin. Was—it. . .?'

'True?' Leith queried when he didn't finish. His eyes
were fixed on hers, and he nodded. 'Actually,' she
replied, 'I've—er—never had a lover.' Naylor was looking so dumbstruck that she thought she had better say a

little more. 'You're the nearest,' she added shyly, 'I've ever come to. . .'

'Oh, you darling!' he groaned. 'Come here.' Tenderly he gathered her up close, and tenderly he planted loving gentle kisses all over her face. 'Oh, my darling,' he muttered again, 'that makes my behaviour so much worse!'

'I. . . I'm not with you,' she told him huskily, and was held by him quietly for long, long moments. Then, only when he had held her as though to say that nothing would ever harm her again if he could help it, did he begin to explain.

'That night, when my aunt and uncle came back from the stables, I came to my senses a little and returned to my room—to spend one of the most mortifying nights of my life!'

'Mortifying?' she questioned, knowing all about her own mortification that night but not thinking for a moment that he'd suffered in the same way.

'What else? You'd known at least one lover, or so I believed, but I'd observed a fine sensitivity in you which made me instinctively feel that you were more extremely selective in your choice of partners than promiscuous. You'd told me yourself how you came to leave your previous job, so I knew full well how badly you were shaken when that oaf Ardis made a grab for you. Likewise you were shaken when that lout Fisher tried something similar. Then, before you'd barely recovered from that,' he went on solemnly, 'here am I—who love you so much that in my saner, non-jealous moments, am ready to protect you with my life—making a grab for you too and frightening you half to death. Can you wonder that when I came to my senses, I was so mortified I decided to cut our weekend short?'

'Was that the reason?' Leith exclaimed in astonishment. 'I sort of had an idea we might be staying a few hours longer, but. . .'

'I'd intended to leave after lunch, but my decision was made before I saw you on Sunday morning and you went scarlet. I was again mortified that your high colour could only have come from the alarm you still felt. It confirmed for me that I should take you where you felt safe. I later wanted to—tried to, in fact, tell you that you didn't need to be afraid of me. . .'

'I wasn't afraid of you!' Leith assured him quickly. 'I know I went red that Sunday, but. . .but—well, it's—um—not every day—um—night that I cuddle up to a man when I'm—er—nearly n-naked.'

'Shyness!' he exclaimed incredulously. Then, his expression softening, 'Oh, my little love, you were shy that no man had ever seen you like that before! Oh, come close to me,' he breathed, and held her to him, rubbing his face against her hair.

'I don't think I was ever that afraid of you,' Leith, her voice husky with emotion, thought it only fair she should tell him. 'Only last Monday you held me in your arms and it was pure joy for me.'

'For you too?' he murmured, then revealed, 'You clung to me and I thought you might hear my heart pounding, because this time your clinging to me wasn't phoney as it was when my aunt and uncle were there. But my heart was pounding for another reason too last Monday.'

'What other reason?' Leith had to know.

'I knew you for a sensitive but gutsy woman,' he obliged happily. 'Yet I'd seen hurt in your face when I quite abominably suggested you had an interest in my financial standing. My heart began to thump as I wondered, could it be that I had the power to hurt you? Did that mean, then, that you had some feeling, however small, for me?'

'What did you decide?' Leith asked, moving her head so she could see his face.

'I didn't have a chance to decide anything before Travis showed up and I was once again being eaten alive by jealousy and suspicion. It was of no help at all, woman,' he growled, 'to come to your flat that night and have you tell me that Travis would always be someone special to you. I couldn't take it, I had to get out of there before I did something desperate.'

'Oh, darling!' Leith cried, 'I only said what I did because I was afraid you might have seen, from the way I'd been that morning—the way I was in no hurry to leave your arms—who it was I *did* love.'

'You witch!' he told her lovingly, but, going on, 'Then the very next day, to add to the injury, when I was so much in love with you that I couldn't bear the thought of not having you where I could find you, where I could see you, you had the unmitigated nerve to hand in your notice!'

'You soon sorted me out, though, didn't you?' she laughed.

'You're darn right I did.' He grinned. 'But only to spend the next couple of days in determining that, whether I had to have you where I could see you or not, I wasn't going out of my way for the privilege.'

'Really?'

'Fact,' he replied, but had to grin again as he owned, 'After which nose-cutting-off exercise, I was going quite demented by Friday for a sight of you.'

'But we saw each other in the corridor yesterday morning. You ignored me,' she recalled easily.

'I should go out of my way to speak to someone who obviously had no intention of speaking!' Naylor counter-accused. 'After I'd come looking for you, too!'

'Honestly?' she gasped.

'Honestly,' he confirmed. 'All of which went to make me realise that I couldn't take not seeing you over the weekend. I've never been lovesick before,' he inserted. 'My stars, it's a powerful emotion!'

'Is that why you sent for me yesterday afternoon?'

He nodded. 'I wasn't sure that you'd go for the line that my aunt and uncle wanted to get to know you, but it was the best I could come up with to persuade you to join me this weekend.'

'You were lying!'

'Yes and no,' he answered. 'It's true that my folks want to get to know you—but they never specifically said so.'

'You hound!' She smiled adoringly.

'That's true too,' he accepted cheerfully, though his expression darkened a little as he added, 'But we'd hardly got here than I was again manhandling you when I kissed you in a jealous rage.'

Leith looked at him, and realised the welter of torment he'd been in. 'And I,' she whispered softly, 'when next I saw you, wanted to wipe away what had been—like this.' Gently then, so gently, she stretched up and kissed him.

'Truth?' he asked in some astonishment.

'Gospel,' she smiled.

'Remind me to tell you, daily, what a wonderful woman you are,' Naylor breathed tenderly, and as Leith smiled again, 'I felt then, when you hurtled into your bedroom, that everything had come to a head. I knew I was going to have to take some action, even if I hadn't decided then what form that action would take. But all I knew then was that I felt the best thing I could do would be to keep well away from the vicinity of your bedroom, so I decided, in some despair, I own, to wait for you in the drawing-room. I hardly dared to believe you'd still be wearing my engagement ring when you came looking for my aunt and uncle, but it gave me no end of a lift that you were. Then Travis turned up, and while I was still reeling to see he'd got an arm round some other woman who he was claiming he was going to marry, you did a disappearing act.'

'You soon found me,' Leith stated.

'Too right,' Naylor replied stoutly, and, bringing her left hand up to his mouth, he kissed her ringed finger.

'I'll—er—let you have it back,' she murmured a little awkwardly.

'What?'

'The ring.'

'Don't you like it? If you don't I'll——'

'It isn't that,' she interrupted quickly. 'It's beautiful. It's just that, since we're not engaged, I wouldn't want you to——'

'Not engaged! Ye gods, Leith, what in thunder do you think I've been talking about for this past half-hour if not the fact that you and I are going to be married as soon as we possibly can?'

'Married. . .?' she choked. 'Are w-we?'

'Are you saying we're not?' Naylor demanded in his old forthright way.

It took Leith less than a second to reply. 'Of course not,' she answered.

'You're going to marry me?' Naylor, it seemed, still wanted the I's dotted and the T's crossed.

'You're sure?'

'I'm sure of that above all else,' he told her sternly. 'I was staggered by my strength of feeling when yesterday you dared to state that you were not going to marry me. I knew then that I'd not rest until you were my bride. Now then, give me a straight yes, and stop giving me more grief,' he ordered.

'Yes, sir.' She obeyed promptly, and laughed, and was entirely enraptured when, holding her close, he joined in.

HARLEQUIN ✦ PRESENTS®

BARBARY WHARF

An exciting six-book series, one title per month beginning in October, by bestselling author

Charlotte Lamb

Set in the glamorous and fast-paced world of international journalism, BARBARY WHARF will take you from the *Sentinel*'s hectic newsroom to the most thrilling cities in the world. You'll meet media tycoon Nick Caspian and his adversary Gina Tyrrell, whose dramatic story of passion and heartache develops throughout the six-book series.

In book one, BESIEGED (#1498), you'll also meet Hazel and Piet. Hazel's always had a good word to say about everyone. Well, almost. She just can't stand Piet Van Leyden, Nick's chief architect and one of the most arrogant know-it-alls she's ever met! As far as Hazel's concerned, Piet's a twentieth-century warrior, and she's the one being besieged!

Don't miss the sparks in the first BARBARY WHARF book, BESIEGED (#1498), available in October from Harlequin Presents.

BARB-S

WELCOME TO

The quintessential small town, where everyone knows everybody else!

Finally, books that capture the pleasure of tuning in to your favorite TV show!

GREAT READING...GREAT SAVINGS...AND A FABULOUS FREE GIFT!

Each book set in Tyler is a self-contained love story; together, the twelve novels stitch the fabric of the community. The covers honor the old American tradition of quilting; each cover depicts a patch of the large Tyler quilt.

With Tyler you can receive a fabulous gift, ABSOLUTELY FREE, by collecting proofs-of-purchase found in each Tyler book. And use our special Tyler coupons to save on your next TYLER book purchase.

Join your friends at Tyler for the seventh book, ARROWPOINT by Suzanne Ellison,
available in September.

Rumors fly about the death at the old lodge! What happens when Renata Meyer finds an ancient Indian sitting cross-legged on her lawn?

Back by Popular Demand

Janet Dailey
Americana

Janet Dailey takes you on a romantic tour of America through fifty favorite Harlequin Presents novels, each one set in a different state and researched by Janet and her husband, Bill.

A journey of a lifetime. The perfect collectible series!

September titles
#39 RHODE ISLAND
   Strange Bedfellow
#40 SOUTH CAROLINA
   Low Country Liar

JAYNE ANN KRENTZ

A two-part epic tale from one of today's most popular romance novelists!

Dreams
Parts One & Two

The warrior died at her feet, his blood running out of the cave entrance and mingling with the waterfall. With his last breath he cursed the woman—told her that her spirit would remain chained in the cave forever until a child was created and born there....

So goes the ancient legend of the Chained Lady and the curse that bound her throughout the ages—until destiny brought Diana Prentice and Colby Savager together under the influence of forces beyond their understanding. Suddenly they were both haunted by dreams that linked past and present, while their waking hours were filled with danger. Only when Colby, Diana's modern-day warrior, learned to love, could those dark forces be vanquished. Only then could Diana set the Chained Lady free....

 Available in September wherever Harlequin books are sold.